Boardroom to Bedroom

*The way to a man's heart…
is through the bedroom!*

THE BOSS'S MARRIAGE ARRANGEMENT
by Penny Jordan

and

HIS DARLING VALENTINE
by Carole Mortimer

Two original stories to celebrate
Valentine's Day by your favorite Presents authors—
together in one volume!

PENNY JORDAN has been writing for more than twenty years and has an outstanding record: over 130 novels published, including the phenomenally successful *A Perfect Family, To Love, Honour and Betray, The Perfect Sinner* and *Power Play*, which hit the *Sunday Times* and *New York Times* bestseller lists. Penny Jordan was born in Preston, Lancashire, England.

CAROLE MORTIMER was born in England, the youngest of three children. She began writing in 1978, and has now written over ninety books for Harlequin Mills and Boon®. Carole has four sons, Matthew, Joshua, Timothy and Peter. She says, "I'm happily married to Peter Senior. We live on the Isle of Man."

Look out for more titles from these authors coming soon in Harlequin Presents®

Possessed by the Sheikh
by Penny Jordan
#2457
Coming in April

The Vengeance Affair
by Carole Mortimer

Available from our book club in May (#250)
and also available from retail in November
as part of the Secret Passions series
in our Collectors' Edition.

Penny Jordan
Carole Mortimer

BOARDROOM TO BEDROOM

*The way to a man's heart...
is through the bedroom!*

HARLEQUIN®

TORONTO • NEW YORK • LONDON
AMSTERDAM • PARIS • SYDNEY • HAMBURG
STOCKHOLM • ATHENS • TOKYO • MILAN • MADRID
PRAGUE • WARSAW • BUDAPEST • AUCKLAND

ISBN 0-373-12446-5

BOARDROOM TO BEDROOM

First North American Publication 2005.

THE BOSS'S MARRIAGE ARRANGEMENT
Copyright © 2004 by Penny Jordan.

HIS DARLING VALENTINE
Copyright © 2005 by Carole Mortimer.

www.eHarlequin.com

Printed in U.S.A.

Penny Jordan

THE BOSS'S MARRIAGE ARRANGEMENT

CHAPTER ONE

As ALWAYS when she had to walk past her boss's open office door, Harriet felt her body tense and she forced herself to look straight ahead and not into the room.

She should never have agreed to work for Matthew Cole, she admitted, reflecting darkly as she did so that if it hadn't been for her best friend then she wouldn't have done. That was the trouble with best friends; sometimes—too many times, in her experience—they tended to believe that they knew what was best! Her particular best friend certainly did, which was why he had coaxed, cajoled and generally used every trick in the book to get her to submit her CV for Matthew Cole's personal appraisal.

Yes, that was right, her best friend was male! She and Ben had been friends since their junior school days, and that friendship had strengthened when they had both chosen to go to the same university.

Now, four years after they'd left university, their friendship was as strong as ever—which was why she had taken Ben's advice and applied for the job at the firm of architects and design consultants, which he had insisted would be perfect for her.

And, to be fair to him, in all probability it would have been. If the job hadn't come with strings. Strings that were firmly held in the uncompromising grip of the company's owner, Matthew Cole. And strings which Matthew Cole had absolutely no compunction about pulling extremely hard when he felt like it. Take the way he had dictatorially announced that her desk was to be on the opposite side of the room from Ben's, even though they were collaborating on the same office design project.

She should have listened to her own inner feelings right from the start, Harriet admitted, her green eyes shadowing as sunlight spilled through the window, burnishing her conker-coloured shoulder length hair. The thickness of her long black eyelashes gave her eyes a certain smouldering sensuality, which was echoed by the warm fullness of her mouth.

As she passed Mathew Cole's office she let out a sigh of relief. She knew without looking in that he wasn't there. For some reason she had developed a very sensitive early-warning system that told her very explicitly whenever Matt was about.

If she had had any sense she would have paid far more attention to that stab of shocked awareness and its ricocheting fall out when he had first interviewed her. She should have done, but when Ben had asked her jovially if she had been, as he put it, 'knocked out by Matt's sexiness, like every other woman who sets eyes on him,' she had of course denied being so much as remotely aware of any such thing, never mind affected by it!

Ben had been hugely amused by her reaction, shaking his head and laughing as he told her how women normally reacted to his boss. And that had been her downfall. Because of course when she had been offered the job her own pride had not allowed her to refuse to accept it.

Despite the shock that Matthew Coles's potent air of sexuality and masculine power had given her, she was totally immune to it—and to him, Harriet assured herself, with blatant disregard for the truth, as she walked into the open plan office she shared with Ben and other members of their team.

'Nice weekend?' Ben asked as she sat down.

'Fine,' Harriet assured him. 'Everyone at home sends their love, and your mother has sent some of her damson jam for you.'

Ben groaned. 'I've got a shelf full of the stuff already. You'd think that after twenty-six years she'd know I don't like damson jam.'

'Perhaps she's trying to convert you. Which reminds me—she wants to know when she and your dad are going to get to meet Cindi!' Harriet laughed, but her laughter died on her lips as she studied Ben's haggard face.

'What's wrong?' she asked, her concern intensifying as he shook his head. 'Come on, Ben,' she cajoled, 'this is me—remember!'

She hadn't forgotten, even if Ben had, how he had helped and comforted her through the break up of her own first big romance during their first year at university.

'It's Cindi,' Ben admitted unhappily. 'We had a bit of row over the weekend. And it isn't the first one either. Harry, I just don't understand her,' he said vehemently as he swung around in his chair to look at her. 'I mean, one minute she's "let's move in together and start planning a future" and then the next she's saying, "I'm out with my friends and I don't want to know you." And all because...'

'Because what?' she pressed, but Ben shook his

head. Harriet sighed. Cindi, the girl Ben was dating, had recently joined the company too, although since they were working on different projects, and she herself had been away on holiday, Harriet hadn't had any opportunity to get to know her as yet. She knew that Cindi and Ben had been dating, and that they had fallen head over heels in love with one another.

'Everyone has lovers' tiffs, Ben.' She tried to comfort him. 'Perhaps give yourselves a chance to talk the problem through together…?'

'This isn't a tiff. She's being totally unreasonable and she knows it. And as for talking it through—!' His normally easygoing expression hardened. 'No way I am going to be given ultimatums about the way I live my life!'

Harriet could see that he genuinely believed he had a grievance, but she still tried to lighten his mood by teasing, 'What has she done? Told you all your old sports stuff has to go?'

When he didn't respond she looked worriedly at him and said quietly, 'Okay, so it's something serious and I'm out of order trying to joke about it, but you can be a stubborn so-and-so at times, and if it's a matter of giving a bit or losing someone special to you then—'

'It isn't as simple as that, Harry, and if she genuinely loved me she wouldn't need to make such bloody ridiculous conditions because she'd know…'

'She'd know what?' Harriet demanded, mystified.

For a minute she thought that Ben wasn't going to answer, and then, as though he couldn't help himself, he burst out furiously, 'She'd know that you're the closest thing I've got to a sister, as well as my best friend, and that no way do you feel any differently about me than I do about you. Hell, just because she's never had any close friends of the opposite sex doesn't mean that— And as for saying that you might secretly be in love with me—well, that's just plain ridiculous!'

It took Harriet several seconds to assimilate what Ben was telling her, but once she had, she protested immediately, 'She can't possibly think that! You must have misunderstood.'

'I wish!' Ben responded darkly.

'Look, Ben, let me have a word with her,' Harriet offered.

'No. No! It's no use. She won't believe you, Harry. And that's what's really getting to me. I've given her my word that I've been totally up front with her about us, but apparently my word isn't good enough.' His voice hardened. 'What she wants—what she says her friends have told her she should demand—is for me to prove to her that there's nothing going on between you and me by cutting you out of my life completely. She says if I loved her then I'd agree. She says she will not accept me having another woman in my life who means more to me than she does. And she says that if I don't accept her terms then it means that you *do* mean more! I've tried to make her understand— to see...to admit that she's being sexist and stupid, and that if she loved me she would accept my word that she's got it all wrong. After all, I know you a damn sight better than she does. You aren't secretly in love with me, are you?'

Harriet burst out laughing. 'No, I am not!' she assured him truthfully.

From where she stood it was easy for her to see how and why the argument had escalated out of control, even if she did feel affronted by Cindi's assumption that she was the sort of person who would try to break up someone else's romance. Take two people who had fallen passionately in love but who did not know one another all that well, add a generous helping of female jealousy, a pinch of insecurity and a good measure of male pride, and what you had were all the ingredients for a very destructive explosion.

Right now Ben might have an angrily stubborn look in his eyes, but Harriet could see the pain he was trying to hide. Automatically she leaned forward and took hold of his hand, giving it a comforting squeeze.

On his way past the large room which housed his creative design team, Matt Cole came to an abrupt halt as he surveyed the intimacy of the way Harriet was leaning towards Ben and reaching for his hand, her eyes liquid with tender emotion.

Matt was thirty-six years old, the head of his own highly innovative and profitable company, and supposed to be possessed of a sharply astute brain—so why the hell had he not recognised what was happening to him the minute he had set eyes on Harriet and taken immediate and evasive action then?

Because he had believed then, in his arrogance, that he had more than enough power and control over his emotions to keep them in check, that was why. He had felt the immediate fierce surge of emotional and physical reaction to her and dismissed its importance, shrugging it and his own feelings aside, telling himself that it hardly mattered that he happened to find her attractive since he had a rule that he never mixed business with pleasure. And, since he had never previously had any problems in sticking to that rule, he hadn't thought it would pose any problems now.

But he had misjudged the strength of his own feelings. Big time. Very big time.

He was the only child of older parents. His mother had died shortly after his birth, while his father had died when he was in his first year at university, and so all along Matt had focused on his work as a means of providing him with the only kind of security he had told himself he needed.

Marriage and children were on his agenda—eventually. But falling passionately, mindlessly and helplessly in love, and having his whole world turned upside down were not!

But that was exactly what had happened. And, what was more, with every day that passed it was growing harder and harder for him to deal with his feelings.

He had tried to distance himself from Harriet, to cut himself off from what he felt by putting up a façade of cold indifference, but he might as well have tried to breathe without oxygen he acknowledged grimly.

Every day, several times a day, he found himself making some kind of excuse to be in the vicinity of her desk. Every day he watched with a jealousy that made him appalled at himself as she lavished on Ben the attention he longed to have her lavish on him!

He had tried everything, from telling himself he was behaving unprofessionally to telling himself he was behaving ridiculously, but nothing made the slightest difference to what he felt. What he felt right now was that he wanted to stride over to Harriet and take her in his arms and kiss her—if not senseless then at least into a state where she wanted him to the same extent that he wanted her, and to hell with the consequences! But even stronger than his desire to make love to her was his desire to shield and to protect her. To shield her from some of her colleagues' contemptuous and critical comments about her and to protect her from the consequences of her own behaviour.

It made no difference how often he told himself that as one of his employees she had no more right to his protection than any of the others, or that he had no right to want to protect her. He loved her, and he couldn't bear to hear what was being said about her. He found it hard to stand to one side and allow the inevitable to happen. Because everyone, it seemed, believed that sooner or later someone, if not Ben himself, was going to tell her to stop making a fool of herself by displaying so plainly her feelings for a man who obviously did not return them.

If an adult human being had to suffer unrequited love, then better by far that they suffer it in secret—as he was doing.

But what right did he have to interfere? Either as her employer or as the man who loved her?

Morally perhaps none! But emotionally... Matt exhaled sharply.

Helplessly he watched Harriet move even closer to Ben. It was a physical effort to stop himself from going over and separating them.

Didn't she know what a fool she was making of herself? Didn't she care? Didn't she realise that people were discussing her and her obvious love for Ben—a man who saw her only as a friend—behind her back?

Because if she didn't she damned well ought to!

It would take a much braver man than Ben himself to tell her though, Matt recognised, and her female colleagues seemed to prefer to gossip about the situation rather than do anything about it. He had happened to be standing out of sight but well within earshot the previous week, when Cindi had been despairingly confiding in an older woman employee about a row she had had with Ben over his friendship with Harriet.

'He swears that she is nothing more to him than a friend,' Matt had heard her saying tearfully.

'Well, he may see their relationship that way, but it's obvious that she doesn't,' her companion had retorted darkly. 'Look at the way she's followed him here! Don't make the same mistake I did, Cindi,' she had warned her. 'My ex swore to me that his secretary meant nothing to him, but, as the little tart told me the day he left me for her, she wanted him and nothing was going to stop her having him. Some women are like that! And if you want my opinion Harriet is one of them! I mean, you've only got to see her with Ben. It's obvious how she feels about him. She spends every spare minute she can with him. Take it from me, she wants him—no matter what he might say or think!'

'Don't, please,' Cindi had protested. 'Ben says he loves me, but...'

'Then tell him to prove it! Tell him that you want her out of his life!'

But Harriet very plainly was *not* out of Ben's life, and had no intention of getting out of it.

Didn't she realise what people were saying? Didn't she care that Ben was actually seeing something else? Had she no pride, no sense of self-respect or self-worth? Hadn't it occurred to her to stop obsessing about Ben and find a man who loved and wanted her? Matt wondered angrily.

A man?

His mouth compressing, he wondered helplessly for the thousandth time why this had had to happen to him! It wasn't what he wanted, and it sure as hell wasn't what he needed! It felt as if his jealousy was burning a hole in his gut.

Cynically he reflected that a sitcom writer would have a field-day, if not a whole carnival with the situation!

Matt loves Harriet, who loves Ben, who loves Cindi, who loves Ben, who does not love Harriet, who does not love Matt, who does love her—with the kind of savage, self-destructive, all-consuming hunger that set all his inner emotional buttons on overdrive and meltdown every damned time he saw her. And it didn't help that every damned time he *did* see her she was draping herself on or around Ben!

And what in some ways was even worse was the fact that Matt knew that if he were Ben, business ethics and self-imposed rules or not, he'd have had her in his arms, his mouth on hers, faster than she could blink. He drew in a deep, shuddering breath and fought for self-control.

Ignobly and impossibly he had even at one stage contemplated firing her. But, even if the law hadn't prevented him from doing any such thing without a watertight reason, she was far too much of an asset to the business for it to lose her.

And that was just one of the more minor reasons why he loved her. Unlike Ben, who was a good, solid and cheerful worker, Harriet had brought a passion and flair to her role in the team that had infused the project she was working on with a new dynamism.

It wasn't that he hadn't tried to overcome his feelings for her; he had! In the past few months he had dated more women than he had done in the past few years. But none of them had so much as dragged his thoughts away from Harriet for as long as five seconds.

Her Matt-aware antennae for once not working efficiently, Harriet was oblivious to the fact that Matt could overhear her as she shook her head and told Ben firmly, 'We can't talk about this here.' Giving his hand another squeeze, she suggested, 'Why don't we have dinner together tonight? I've got loads to tell you about what's going on at home.'

Watching her, Matt felt as though someone was ripping his heart, muscle from muscle. He wanted to stride over to them, to take hold of Harriet and ask her if she realised what she was doing. And then what? Force her to back off and allow Ben and Cindi to get on with their lives—and their love?

He had no right to interfere, he warned himself harshly. But if he didn't then who would? And besides, a dangerously reasonable little voice inside him argued, didn't he have the right as an employer to want a workplace free of any emotional entanglements and dramas that would take his employees' attention away from their work?

Oblivious to what Matt was thinking, Harriet watched Ben. He looked so dejected that she felt desperately sorry for him, and wanted to do whatever she could to help. Cindi obviously loved Ben, and Harriet knew that Ben loved Cindi. She was amazed that Ben had even needed to ask her if she was secretly in love with him! How could she be when…? When what? When she was desperately afraid that she had fallen in love with Matt?

Matt! Automatically she lifted her head and looked towards the corridor which led to his office, her body stiffening and hot colour staining her skin as she saw him standing watching them.

Ben was a good looking young man, but he was just that—a young man. In no way did he compare in sheer male presence to Matthew Cole, who was pure lethal adult, and so fully charged with testosterone that no woman living could fail to be aware of him. Not that she didn't do her bit for her own sex by fiercely pretending that she was not. She *was* aware of him. All the time! But some days, sometimes—like right now—something went wrong and her protective shield failed to work properly. Sometimes just the sight of Matt was enough to set up a chain of reaction inside her body that resulted in butterflies in her tummy and a weakness in her legs. But that weakness was nowhere near as dangerous as the weakness in her emotions.

Because the truth was that Matt epitomised everything Harriet had ever dreamed about in a man. He was her childhood prince come to life; her knight in shining armour. He was her darkly disturbing, secret sensual-fantasymade man. He made her ache with feverish longing—and, far more dangerously, he made her dream impossible daydreams about love and happy ever afters, and at least four little Matts or Matildas calling her Mummy!

And no way was that ever going to happen! Matt didn't even like her, never mind love her. In fact sometimes when he was looking at her the way he was right now, his slate-grey eyes iced with permafrost and freezing her with the most intimidating glare of fury she had ever seen, she felt that he actively disliked her.

Her heart might be sinking, Harriet acknowledged, but her chin wasn't going to. Bravely she tilted it, and met his slicing scrutiny.

What was it about the thickness of his close-cropped dark hair that made her want to slide her fingers into it, to mould them against the curve of his well-shaped head, whilst one of his strong hands cupped her own, and that hard mouth softened with desire and…?

'Harriet, I'd like to see you in my office.'

The cold, clinical words brought her back to earth.

'You mean now?' she queried. She needed to keep her distance from him right now, not get even closer to him. Harriet had her pride—the same pride that had led to her refusing to give in to her first love's demand that she go to bed with him—and she was not going to join the ranks of Matt's lovelorn adorers.

'I mean now!' he agreed, in a clipped voice that made Ben give her a small shove.

'See you tonight, then,' he said.

Matt had already disappeared down the corridor, and as she followed him Harriet wondered feverishly what he wanted.

There had never been any open clashes between them. How could there be when he was not just her immediate boss but the owner of the company as well? But there had been plenty of subtle indirect ones.

It wasn't so much Matt's antagonism towards her that sparked off the fiery pride that led to her spirited defiance but her own shocked stark inner awareness of just how vulnerable to him she was.

Apart from the brief catastrophe of her first foray into love Harriet had remained heart-whole, and that was the way she had intended to remain until she was well into her thirties and ready to settle down. And then she had seen Matt and her sensible plans had self-ignited after one incredulous look at him. Nor had it made any difference telling herself that no sensible and right-thinking woman would be so idiotic as to fall crazily in love with a man who obviously was never going to feel the same way about her.

Abruptly Harriet realised that she had reached Matt's office.

An inimical biting grey glance impaled her where she stood, leaving her feeling as though her every thought had been dissected and then rejected.

'Come in and close the door.'

Her heart was going crazy inside her chest. But it wasn't her erratic heartbeat that bothered her as she mentally cursed herself for leaving her jacket on her chair.

The state-of-the-art office had a climatically controlled temperature that made it totally unnecessary for her nipples to do some temperature-awareness testing of their own. But that was exactly what they were doing—pressing themselves against her clothes for the entire world to see, as though she was standing in an arctic wind.

Or sexually aroused. Well, she certainly knew

which it was, and she could only hope that Matt did *not!*

Her nipples tightened so fiercely that she almost cried out in protest.

'Sit down.'

Woodenly, Harriet did so.

For once Matt had no carefully thought out plan of action mentally organised. He only knew that for her own sake Harriet needed to distance herself from Ben—both in her own emotions and in other people's eyes.

The intensity of his grim expression as he battled with his own private devils increased Harriet's apprehension. What on earth had she done?

'It's come to my attention that your...feelings for Ben are the subject of a great deal of office criticism and gossip.'

Harriet could feel the tips of her ears starting to burn hotly in mortified shock. Matt had swung his chair around so that she could only see his profile, but she was miserably and humiliating aware that he could still see how his words were affecting her.

Her whole face was burning now, with both anger and humiliation, as the full ramifications of his accusatory and demeaning statement sank in.

Immediately she rushed to defend herself, and to reject what he was saying. 'If you are referring to Cindi's ridiculous suggestion that I am secretly in love with Ben—'

'Secretly?' Matt stopped her sharply, turning to face her. 'There was nothing secret about the touching little scene I just witnessed. Touching, that is, unless one happens to know the truth! And the entire company knows the truth, Harriet.' The look Matt gave her made her want to disappear!

Through stiff, shock-numbed lips Harriet managed to demand, 'And that truth is…?'

There was a look in her eyes that made Matt want to go to her and hold her, tell her that nothing and no one was going to be allowed to hurt her whilst he was there to prevent it, but he knew that he couldn't. He was doing this because he wanted to help her, not because he wanted to hurt her!

'That you are refusing to see that your love for Ben is not returned, that it never will be returned. The way you are pursuing him so obsessively, following him and clinging to him, is not only coming between him and Cindi, it's making you the object of other people's contempt as well.'

The cold, brutal words hit her like physical blows, and as from physical blows Harriet recoiled from them, whispering painfully, 'No, that isn't true.'

'It *is* true. Have you no pride? No self-respect?'

The blood receded swiftly from Harriet's face, leaving it creamily pale as shock and outrage filled her.

Cindi's assumption and Cindi's ultimatum had obviously not been confined merely to Ben! It was bad enough discovering that her colleagues shared Cindi's misinterpretation of her relationship with Ben, but to discover that Matt was not just privy to it but believed it as well filled her with blistering hot shame.

Valiantly she struggled to overcome her feelings and to explain. After all, no matter what her private feelings might be, Matt was her boss, and at this stage in her career she couldn't afford to earn any kind of black mark, still less be written off as some kind of obsessive who was trying to force herself on a man who didn't want her!

'I was just trying to tell Ben—'

'What?' Matt challenged her, striding from behind his desk and coming over to her. 'What were you trying to tell him? That he'd be better off with you? With your love?'

'No!'

'No? So what, then? Were you pleading with him to love *you?*'

'No! *No!*' Harriet denied fiercely, getting to her own feet to confront him and then wishing that she hadn't as she realised how close to him she was.

She wasn't a small woman, at five feet nine inches tall, but she was small-boned and slender, and Matt was well over six feet, with a physique which Ben had told her came from his days as captain of his university's rugby team.

How on earth had this happened? How could she possibly be in this sickeningly humiliating situation?

Matt could see the pain in her eyes. Part of him felt bitterly angry with her for what she was doing, but most of him simply wanted to hold her and comfort her. Her pain was his pain, and he hurt for her and with her.

It was simply to comfort her that he had put his hands on her and drawn her towards him. Nothing more!

Harriet stiffened as Matt's hands closed on her upper arms, knowing that right now she was far too emotionally frail to withstand something like this.

Ben was forgotten as though he had never existed. She tried to drag air into lungs compressed with shocked physical awareness.

Matt was touching her. Matt was looking down into her eyes with frowning bleakness.

She exhaled shakily.

He shouldn't have done this. He shouldn't have touched her, Matt recognised grimly. No matter how altruistic his original motivation and intention had been. Abruptly he released her.

As Matt thrust her away Harriet tensed, hating herself for the way she wanted—no, not just wanted, but ached and needed—to cling to him.

'Quite apart from anything else,' she could hear Matt telling her grimly, 'your behaviour is causing disruption and…and discord here in the office. And that is something I will not tolerate. We work together here, in very tight-knit teams, and every single member of those teams has been selected by me personally as a vital component of their particular unit. But if I thought it necessary for the greater good to replace one of those components then I would have no compunction whatsoever in doing so. Do you understand what I am saying?'

'Yes, you're threatening to sack me,' Harriet answered him briefly. 'But you've got it all wrong! And so has Cindi! I do love Ben, yes! But as a friend…as a brother, if you like. Not…not in the way that you are trying to imply!'

'You mean there's nothing sexual in your… your…?'

'Nothing,' Harriet emphasised fiercely, without letting him finish.

'No?' Matt gave her a cynical look that made her whole body burn with resentment. 'Then prove it,' he told her in a clipped voice.

Harriet exhaled noisily. 'And how exactly am I supposed to do that?'

'Well, you could start by making it obvious and public that you're very involved with.. dating someone else.'

'Dating someone else?' Harriet repeated blankly. 'Who?'

'Me!'

The colour came and went in Harriet's mobile face—and if she had but known it her shock only echoed his own, Matt acknowledged. What the hell did he think he was doing? Morally and in every other way there was he was totally out of order. He should make it clear immediately that he hadn't meant what he had said and that Harriet was to ignore it. *Immediately!*

Matt was suggesting that she pretend to want him? No pretence was necessary!

'You can't mean... Are you saying...? Oh, no, I couldn't do that. It's impossible... No. No way!' she told him a little breathlessly.

Her words didn't just sting Matt's pride raw, they blew a large hole in his good intentions as well as shattering them into nothing. A ruthless determination swept over him, swamping everything else.

'You've just said that you aren't in love with Ben—I'm giving you an opportunity to prove it.'

There was a small suspenseful pause.

'If you don't take it then I'll know that you are lying,' Matt finished coldly.

Harriet looked at him, wondering how on earth she had ever got into such a mess.

'No one will ever believe that you and I are dating.'

'Then it will be up to us to convince them, won't it?' Matt said smoothly. 'The choice is yours!'

'Some choice,' Harriet muttered, adding fiercely, 'Why are you doing this?'

Her throat felt raw, the backs of her eyes stung, and her chest hurt, as though she were about to come down with a heavy cold. Her physical reactions weren't caused by a physical virus, though, but an emotional one.

'I'm doing it to stop you causing disruption and discord in my business. Besides, I should have thought that if you genuinely don't love Ben, as you claim, then you'd jump at the chance to prove it—and to give Ben and Cindi a chance to find happiness together,' Matt reiterated curtly.

No way could he tell her that he was doing it purely and simply because he wanted any excuse to be with her...

'What was all that about?'

Harriet gave a nervous look over her shoulder as Ben came up to her at the water cooler.

'What...what do you mean?' she hedged.

'What did Matt want? You were in there for ages, and when you came out you looked...'

For a moment she was tempted to tell him, but before she could say anything she heard Matt saying smoothly behind her, 'Have you told Ben about us yet, darling?'

Harriet almost dropped the cup of water she was holding, but she suspected that the shock on her face was nothing to the stupefaction on Ben's as Matt came between them.

'Harry?' Ben questioned incredulously.

'You're trembling. I hope that's because of me,' Matt was murmuring against her ear as he relieved her of the paper cup she had all but crushed by sliding one hand around her waist to turn her towards him and removing the cup with the other.

Ben was positively goggling at them, his mouth half open and a look of total shock on his face.

'You mean, you two are...?' He shook his head.

'We certainly are,' Matt assured him calmly. 'In fact we very much are—aren't we, Harriet?'

The look he was giving her was practically a physical caress in itself, Harriet recognised weakly, and her wretched body was certainly responding to it as though it were.

Ben obviously hadn't missed the high octane sensuality of the smoky look Matt was giving her, because suddenly he started to frown—an expression that Harriet recognised all too well.

Ben was her friend, but he was also male, and as such he had always taken a very brotherly and protective attitude towards Harriet where other men were concerned. And right now he was looking at Matt as though he was a suspicious father about to demand to know Matt's intentions!

'You never said anything to me!' he accused Harriet sternly.

'I asked her not to,' Matt answered promptly for her.

Somehow the hand which had relieved her of the paper cup was now holding her own, his fingers sliding between hers in a manner so intimate that Harriet was having trouble breathing properly. Her skin tingled, and liquid pleasure shot up her arm like an injection of some kind of sensual drug that locked into her heart.

She had the strongest need not just to move closer to Matt's body, but also to press herself against him with wanton abandonment.

Wicked images of the two of them alone together somewhere very private filled her head in a dangerously explicit slide show. Matt perching on the edge of a desk, his legs open as he drew her to him to kiss her passionately, whilst her fingers explored the hard muscles of his thigh, her touch making him growl in protest and take her hand and place it on the swollen bulge of his erection. Whilst he was kissing her he would slowly unfasten her top and remove it. His hands would cup her breasts and savour their shape and feel as her tight, erect nipples flaunted their eager hunger for his touch... Abruptly Harriet called her thoughts to order as she heard, 'But now that things are serious between us it's different. I don't care who knows how I feel about Harriet!'

'Things are serious between you?' Ben's frown cleared, leaving him looking both relieved and happy.

CHAPTER TWO

'HARRIET, I don't understand you! There's Matt telling me that things are serious between the two of you and you haven't said a word! Why not?'

'Er…well, until he called me into his office I didn't know that things were serious,' Harriet explained, mentally justifying her statement by reminding herself that it was the truth after all—if not in the way that Ben would interpret it.

'Well, once Cindi knows this she's going to—'

'Be very relieved,' Harriet finished firmly for him, adding, 'If you love her as much as I think you do, Ben, you won't make an issue of this silly mistake about me. After all, if she didn't love you she wouldn't care about my relationship with you, would she?'

'No… But…' He gave a small sigh. 'She had a few days' holiday to use and she's gone to see her parents—cooling off time, she called it.'

'Well, if I were you I'd be waiting for her when she comes back with something very romantic planned.'

'Yes. I'll do that.' He paused, and then said worriedly, 'Harry, this thing between you and Matt… Don't rush into…anything, will you? I mean, you haven't… He hasn't… And Matt is…'

Oh, yes! Matt most certainly was, Harriet agreed

mentally as she told Ben lightly, 'You worry about your own love life, Ben, and leave me to worry about mine.'

Smiling at him, she leaned forward and kissed his cheek.

Within seconds the phone on her desk rang, and when Harriet picked up the receiver she heard Matt saying coldly, 'I've booked a table for us at the Riverside for nine p.m. I'll pick you up. And by the way, I thought I'd made it clear there's only one man you kiss from now on and it isn't Ben!'

Harriet wanted to tell him that there was no way she intended to have dinner with him, but he had already ended the call. Silently she replaced the receiver. Her head was whirling and her heart was pounding at the thought of what had happened.

Matt had asked her if she wanted people to believe that she was secretly in love with Ben, and of course she didn't. But the cure he was offering her was far, far more dangerous than the supposed disease!

And how ridiculous it was for him to go to the lengths of taking her out to dinner just to stop her seeing Ben, as she had planned. Her heart gave a funny little jerk as it threw itself against her ribcage. She acknowledged that there was a certain dangerous pleasure in the thought of Matt having the kind of feelings about her that would cause him to feel jealous of her being with another man. Not that he was ever likely to!

The Riverside was the area's most exclusive hotel, and was run by an ex-TV chef and his model wife. What on earth was she going to wear? And what on earth was she doing worrying about what she was

going to wear when she had so much that was far
more important to worry about?

Displacement therapy, that was what it was! And
nothing whatsoever to do with any wild and totally
idiotic desire to have Matt take one look at her and
wish that he was serious about her for real!

Matt stared out of the large window of his penthouse
suite above the office block. He had bought the suite
because it saved time to live and work in the same
building, and he'd hired a turnkey designer to sort out
the décor for him. The result was a state-of-the-art
modern living space in which he constantly felt as
though he was somehow a jarring and unnecessary
presence, breaking up the place's austere and sterile
symmetry of grey on grey, chrome, glass and granite.

Harriet would, of course, be fiercely contemptuous
of it—and no doubt of him for living in it. He just
somehow knew that she was an Aga and comfortable
country house kind of woman. And somewhere deep
down Matt suspected that a part of him was dangerously close to being an Aga and country house kind
of man, with four children, who chose to work at
home so that he could be with them...

Because of Harriet? Matt started to frown. Why the
hell had he fallen in love with her? *How* the hell had
he fallen in love with her? He'd only had to look at
her to know what that red hair and passionate energy
were going to mean! And that was without the com-
plication of her blinkered fixation on a man who
didn't want her. If he had any sense he would... He
would what? Turn his back and walk away from her?

So why the hell was he sitting here reliving the feel
of that thick silky waterfall of hair running through

his fingers and the effect of those awesome green eyes looking up into his?

If he hadn't had the presence of mind to push her away there was no knowing what might have happened. No knowing? Matt derided himself savagely—he knew damn well what would have happened: what he had wanted to happen and where he had wanted to have it happen!

It had stunned Matt when a male business associate had commented enviously on his 'playboy' reputation, remarking on the number of women Matt was known to have dated. It had never occurred to him that the method he had chosen of trying to eliminate his feelings for Harriet would result in him gaining the reputation of a would-be stud! The truth about his supposed 'reputation' was that it was largely unfounded.

His recent succession of dinner dates had been just that—dinner dates! And by his choice! In fact he couldn't remember the last time...

Restlessly he got up and walked over to the large window with its view of the city.

Liar, he goaded himself mentally. Of course he could damn well remember. And he could remember too that halfway through dinner he had suddenly looked at his elegant blonde-haired companion and realised with a savage stab of anger that he was both totally unaroused by her and totally bored with her.

That had been the evening after he had interviewed Harriet for the job. His date had been none too pleased to be returned home instead of being taken to bed, and she had let him know it!

Matt frowned as he heard his intercom buzz.

Striding over to it, he flipped it on.

'Matt, it's Ben. I need to talk with you.'

Matt hesitated briefly before answering, 'Fine—come up, Ben.'

As he opened the door to him Matt could see the way Ben looked admiringly around the apartment.

'This is way cool, Matt,' he enthused. 'But Harry won't like it—' he began, then stopped, looking self-conscious.

'It's okay, Ben. I know this place isn't to Harriet's taste,' Matt offered, intending to reassure him, but to his surprise Ben suddenly started to scowl fiercely.

'Harriet's been up here, then, has she?' he demanded, looking pugnacious.

'We *are* dating,' Matt answered obliquely, an unfamiliar and unwanted sensation of having been wrong-footed suddenly hitting him.

Ben's current attitude was not exactly that of a young man who resented Harriet's emotional dependence on him and wanted her taken off his hands at any cost.

'It's about Harry that I came to see you,' Ben told him determinedly, giving Matt the kind of look he last remembered receiving from the very protective father of the girl he had taken to his first school dance.

'I see. Would you like to sit down? Or is it going to be a short conversation?' Matt asked drily.

A tinge of colour darkened Ben's face, but his jaw was still set stubbornly. He had come up here for a purpose and he wasn't going to leave until he had a reassured himself on Harriet's behalf. She was his best friend, after all, and, knowing what he did about his own sex, he wanted to make sure she would be all right.

'Harry hasn't said much about how things got going between the two of you…' he began. 'In fact, I wouldn't have thought she was your type. I've known her since we were kids, and she's my best friend.' Ben stopped, took a deep breath, then began again. 'You said you were serious about Harriet and I hope that you mean that, Matt, because Harry just isn't the type of woman who would let a man into her life in a personal sort of way if she didn't care a hell of a lot about him. She was pretty badly hurt by a rat of a guy when we were at university. Luckily she had the sense to listen to me when I warned her about him, so things never went too far, if you know what I mean. Of course I know it isn't anyone's business but their own how many partners a person has had, and I don't suppose I'd be all that pleased myself if I found I'd got a virgin on my hands…' Matt pressed on doggedly.

A virgin! Ben was trying to tell him that Harriet was a virgin?

Two vastly different emotions speared through Matt at the same time. One was a savage protective fury with Harriet for loving Ben to the extent that she did—ridiculously, in this day and age, she was saving herself for him—and the other was a fierce and disgraceful thrill of hot male hunting instinct. An assured and certain determination to ensure that he was the one who released Harriet from the sensual imprisonment of her virginity.

'So you see,' Ben was continuing, 'if your intentions towards her aren't honourable, so to speak, then it would be better—'

'Ben,' Matt interrupted him firmly, 'I can assure you that my intentions are very honourable.'

'You mean...commitment...? Marriage?' Ben questioned.

Matt's mouth compressed.

'Yes, I mean just that,' he agreed. He meant it, all right, he recognized—after all, he couldn't be any more emotionally committed to her than he was. She already occupied his thoughts 24/7, and as for marriage...

As for marriage! His heart lurched against his ribs and pain tore into him. If circumstances had been different, if Harriet had felt about him as he did about her, then of course he would be wanting marriage, Matt acknowledged grimly. And so, he damned well hoped, after what Ben had just told him, would she!

'You do? Oh, well, that's all right then!'

Beaming with delight, Ben got to his feet to shake Matt's hand. 'Great girl is Harry,' he assured him enthusiastically. 'Good sense of humour, great legs. Must say I was worried... I thought you might just be... Well, I thought I'd better warn you that Harriet isn't that sort of woman.'

No, she wasn't. And Matt decided grimly that he suspected he knew why!

'Thank you, Ben,' he said, dismissing his guest.

Half an hour later, when Harriet opened her door to Matt's knock, the great legs were in evidence but the sense of humour was not.

Not that Matt was in the best of moods himself. The fierce sexual elation he had felt at being told that Harriet was a virgin had given way to an equally fierce and savage fury that she should be idiotic enough to want to save herself for Ben. Ben who did not want her and who, quite plainly, was not right for her! It was, Matt had decided, just the kind of ill-judged, crazy thing a stubborn woman like her would do—saving the gift of herself as well as her love for just one man.

Of course if *he* had been the man…

Harriet took a step back in the hallway as she saw the way Matt was glaring at her. No doubt in his eyes she didn't come anywhere near matching the sophisticated elegance of the women he normally took out to dinner. Her dress was four years old, a simple basic black crêpe number which up until now she had always felt she looked quite good in. With it she was wearing her one pair of expensive shoes, high-heeled and, if she was honest, just a little bit uncomfortable.

'Do you live here alone?' Matt demanded, frowning as he looked up and down the narrow dark lane.

'Yes, I do,' Harriet confirmed. 'I shared with Ben at university, but—'

'Now he wants his own space?' Matt broke in, without allowing her to finish.

Angrily Harriet tilted her chin and told him firmly, 'Actually, I am the one who wanted my own space. And my own washing machine and my own bed!' she added pithily, remembering how much it had infuriated her to return from a visit somewhere, pre-Cindi, to find that one of Ben's mates had 'borrowed' her bed in her absence.

Matt's mouth compressed. When was she going to see sense and accept that Ben did not want her?

'If you're trying to convince me that you shared Ben's bed you're wasting your time,' he told her angrily.

Immediately Harriet stepped back into the house,

but as she reached for the door to turn and slam it Matt guessed what she was about to do and grabbed hold of her wrist.

'Look, why won't you face up to the truth? What is it about you that makes it so hard for you to accept that Ben doesn't want you?' he demanded brutally.

If she really had loved Ben the way Matt seemed to think she did his words would have been unbelievably hurtful and cruel, Harriet decided. 'What is it about *you* that makes you think you've got the right to tell me what to do?' she countered, trying to get her wrist back.

'I've told you what my motivation is,' Matt answered, refusing to release her.

'And I'm telling you that you are barking up the wrong tree. I do not love Ben other than as a friend!'

'How can you say that when—'

'When what?' Harriet challenged when Matt suddenly stopped speaking.

'When you can't string a sentence together without including his name in it,' Matt said evasively.

What the hell was happening to him? He had almost blurted out what Ben had told him.

'We'd better make tracks, otherwise we'll be late,' he added curtly.

Harriet glared at him. 'If you think I'm going to have dinner with you now—'

She gasped as Matt tugged on her wrist and closed the space between them.

'If you think that you aren't...' he retorted softly.

It must be the fact that she was not wearing a coat, coupled with the evening air, that was making her tremble so much, Harriet decided dizzily. But the truth was that it was the musky male scent of Matt's

skin playing havoc with her senses, making her want
to bury her face against him and breathe it and him
into her. She wanted to burrow against his warmth,
she wanted…

A shudder ripped through her, causing Matt to
curse under his breath and drag her into his arms,
holding her hard against his body as he lifted his hand
to cup her face and take possession of her mouth.

Right now, more than anything else, he wanted to
take her back into the house, carry her upstairs and
remove every piece of clothing from her body so that
he could show her just what a fool she was for wasting her time wanting Ben when she could have him.
That scent she was wearing was driving him crazy,
making him feel so damned horny…

Harriet moaned excitedly beneath the hot, thrilling
thrust of his tongue. Her fingers dug into the hardness
of his shoulders as pleasure exploded inside her like
a firework, showering her with golden starbusts of
erotic sensation. She could feel his hand in the thick
softness of her hair, his thumb massaging the delicate
over-sensitive spot just behind her ear and sending a
hot zigzag of female arousal jolting right through her.

Just his touch was enough to activate the kind of
ache inside her that she already knew would lead to
a sleepless, wanting night.

She might, thanks to Ben's determined and sometimes unwanted protection, be the oldest virgin in the
whole city, but that did not mean that her body didn't
already know how to respond to the sweet hotness of
the pleasure that could possess and convulse it.

These last months working for Matt had shown her
how easy it was for just the thought of him to activate

that pleasure, and right now her over-stimulated senses were clamouring hungrily for the real thing.

'Why don't we forget dinner?'

Harriet blinked. How had that happened? How had she said the very words she had just been thinking but in Matt's voice?

Matt groaned inwardly as he realised how out of control he was getting. 'Forget I said that!' he told her tersely.

Forget *he* had said it?

'I suppose you thought I was someone else?' Harriet challenged him angrily.

'Just as you wish that I was someone else?' Matt demanded.

Whilst Harriet struggled to regain her composure Matt hurried them both out of her front door and locked it, handing her the keys before he guided her to his parked car.

Harriet was too engrossed in her own thoughts to object to his cavalier control of the situation, along with her door keys. She had wanted Matt to take her to bed! No, Harriet corrected herself. She had wanted to drag Matt upstairs and take him to bed, and she had nearly told him so!

'Look, there's no point in you giving me the silent disapproving treatment because I'm not Ben. Try facing up to reality!'

Harriet didn't trust herself to reply. She just shook her head in silent frustration.

'Good evening, sir, madam. Would you care for a drink in the bar first? Or would you prefer to go straight to your table?'

Matt looked questioningly at Harriet.

'Straight to the table, please,' she answered, rue-fully aware that despite everything she was extremely hungry. And she was also extremely aware of the fact that they were being shown to what had to be one of the restaurant's very best tables, with a little almost private area all to itself. They could see out through the windows over the river and also around the res-taurant, if they wished, and yet at the same time retain their own privacy.

Grimly she wondered how many other women Matt had brought here. An awful lot if the way the head waiter had recognised him was anything to go by, surely?

She had barely completed her chain of thought when Matt suddenly announced, 'I'm surprised that Henri remembered me—it's ages since I last ate here.'

Harriet almost choked on the delicious walnut roll she was eating.

'There wasn't really any need for you to do this, you know,' she said later, when they had given their order and been served with their food. 'After all, Ben isn't going to see us here!'

'Do you wish he could? Do you think it would make him jealous?'

Harriet exhaled fiercely down her nose and put down the glass of wine she had just picked up.

'For the last time, I am *not* in love with Ben. And having him around when I am out on a date is nor-mally the last thing I would want.' When Matt frowned she told him fiercely, 'This may come as a shock to you, but the only way I love Ben is as a brother, and it's as a brother that he behaves when I date anyone—a very over-protective brother at times, and that isn't always what I want!' she added darkly.

She stopped as she realised how much the wine had loosened her tongue and just what she was in danger of saying and to whom!

'In answer to your question, I brought you here to save you from the temptation of going to see Ben,' Matt said curtly, before continuing, 'I don't need to ask why you don't want Ben treating you like a brother. You obviously want him to think of you as a potential lover, not a sister, and because he doesn't, you—'

'You are just misinterpreting what I said to suit your own ends,' Harriet objected angrily. 'That is not what I meant at all.'

They were glaring at one another like two opponents, their argument only brought to an end by the waiter coming to remove their plates for the next course.

CHAPTER THREE

HARRIET stiffened as she saw the look of appreciation and invitation the pretty girl behind the reception desk gave Matt as they left the restaurant. Yet another reason for keeping clear of him, she decided grimly. What woman in possession of all her senses wanted a man who attracted and encouraged the interest of virtually every female he came into contact with?

Not that Matt had encouraged the girl's acquisitive hungry look, Harriet was forced to concede as Matt strode past her obliviously. But that did not alter the fact that if he had done the girl would have leapt to seize the opportunity, Harriet acknowledged.

Courteously Matt placed his hand beneath her elbow to escort her across the car park, rather in the manner that her father adopted towards elderly female members of the family, she reflected darkly.

Her attention was momentarily distracted by the sight of a couple several yards away, wrapped in each other's arms and exchanging the most passionate of kisses as the woman fumbled to unlock the door of the car.

The pounding of Harriet's heart inside her chest was followed by an ache of longing that seemed to seep into every bit of her.

What would it be like to be loved and wanted by Matt like that? Well, whatever it was like she wasn't

going to be the one to find out, she told herself
sharply.

Matt frowned as he glanced down towards Harriet.
She hadn't spoken since before they had left the restaurant—which was, he suspected, quite a record,
since during the rest of the evening she had engaged
in the kind of conversation that had left him reluctantly impressed by its range and depth. Matt wasn't
used to his dates having as keen an interest in world
affairs as he did himself, nor in them being so comfortable and informed in debating them.

Just listening to Harriet gave the words 'verbal
foreplay' a whole new meaning, he decided ruefully.
Certainly he had never expected that he would find
anything erotic in a vigorous discussion about the
merits of a home-based workforce. But then he found
just about everything about Harriet erotic. In fact, she
fascinated him, infuriated him, and just about occupied every one of his waking hours as well as a large
percentage of his sleeping ones. And that meant...

Harriet glowered at Matt as he suddenly and for no
reason at all stood still right in the middle of the car
park.

The couple by the car were still kissing.

Matt followed the direction of her gaze and tugged
grimly on her arm so that she had to look away.

'Stop thinking about it,' he said curtly. 'It's not
going to happen!'

Harriet could feel her face starting to burn with
guilt and chagrin. Had he really guessed so easily how
much she had wished that she were the one being
kissed so passionately, and by him?

'What makes you think I want it to?' she demanded
defensively.

They had reached his car, and as he unlocked it Matt gave her an oblique look. Her full lips were set in a constrained closed line and her green eyes were a mutinous jade.

He opened the passenger door for her, but as she stepped past him he encircled her with the car door and his body.

'Of course you want it to. You're in love, or you think you are. But Ben is not in love with you.'

Ben! Harriet went limp with relief and sagged against the car. Of course—he thought she was in love with Ben!

'But that doesn't stop you wanting to feel his mouth on yours, wanting to…'

The raw sound of Matt's voice jerked her into defensive anger.

If she had been in love with Ben his last words would not have done her any good at all. As it was they were making her want to look at Matt's own mouth as though she were magnetised by it! And not just look at it, she admitted longingly.

'Have you ever thought of writing sex scenes for films?' she asked him, with what she had intended to be sarcasm but which instead sounded more like breathless wonder, Harriet recognised in self-disgust as she scrambled into the car.

To her relief Matt refused to pick up her gauntlet, and started the car instead.

Half an hour later, as they drove through the down-at-heel area where she lived, Harriet could well imagine what Matt must be thinking. But she liked her small house, tucked in cosily with its neighbours, and she liked her long back garden even more.

As though he had read her mind Matt broke his

silence to announce tersely, 'This is a pretty rough area. Not one I would have thought safe for a woman living on her own.'

Yes, it was a bit of a rough area, and following an outbreak of violent incidents she felt increasingly worried about the fact that gangs of youths had begun to roam the local streets, and that if you possessed a car it was not considered wise to park it outside.

But the area still had a certain artisan quaintness about it, and—even more important to Harriet—her little house was affordable and within public transport distance of the office.

She also liked the fact that she had a local butcher and grocery shop, and that most of her elderly neighbours had been born and bred there and so were full of stories of how the area had once been. But now she was seeing it through Matt's eyes, and what she was seeing made her feel both angry and uncomfortable.

Outside a local take away a gang of youths were scuffling and exchanging obscenities. Harriet could see the look Matt was giving them.

She felt obliged to defend them. 'They're only young.'

'And that gives them licence to be foul mouthed?' Matt challenged her. 'Aren't your family concerned about the kind of area you're living in?' he demanded.

Mutinously Harriet turned away from him, pretending not to hear. The truth was that her parents had been dismayed when she had shown them her new home—but she had managed to talk them around.

One of the reasons she had returned home at the weekend had been to wave them off for her father's lecture tour of America. Since her brother and his family lived in New York, Harriet knew how much her parents were looking forward to their visit, and being able to spend some time with their grandchildren.

'Harriet...' Matt began ominously, and then stopped as he turned into her narrow street and they both saw the police car and the ambulance, lights flashing, outside her elderly neighbour's home.

Her own feelings forgotten, Harriet pressed her hand to her mouth in anxiety. Mrs Simmonds was in her late eighties, and had a fund of interesting stories about the past, but Harriet was aware that she had a weak heart and had taken to surreptitiously checking on the elderly lady every day in a way that meant that she did not hurt her pride.

'Oh, no!'

'What the—'

They both spoke at the same time, and Matt stopped his car.

'It's Mrs Simmonds,' Harriet told him shakily as they watched two burly ambulancemen carrying the old lady into the ambulance on a stretcher.

A police officer was already approaching the car.

'What's happened?' Matt asked.

'I'm Mrs Simmonds's neighbour,' Harriet told him, and got out to join Matt and the policeman. 'I know she has a weak heart...'

'Some young thugs broke into her house,' the policeman told them angrily. 'Ransacked the place, they did, and made so much noise that someone across the street rang us. We don't know yet how bad the old lady's injuries are. She's had a very nasty shock, so they're taking her into hospital to keep an eye on her for a couple of days.'

'Why would anyone break into her house? She doesn't have anything to steal,' Harriet protested, pale with alarm. 'She…'

The policeman gave her a pitying look. 'It will be a drug-related crime, miss. They get that desperate for it they'd rob their own grandmother—and often do—'

Harriet shuddered.

The ambulance was already drawing away, and the policeman turned to return to his own car and waiting colleague.

'Right—that's it,' Matt announced as soon as both vehicles had gone. 'No way are you staying here on your own! I'm going to give you two choices,' he told Harriet grimly. 'Either I stay here with you to-night or you come back to my place with me. I don't care which choice you make, but let's put it this way. I only have one bedroom!'

Harriet felt a jolt in her stomach as though someone had kicked her. One bedroom! Already her body was reacting to the sensual mental fantasy she was creating! What would Matt say if she told him she wanted the second option?

'I mean what I say, Harriet!' he said sternly, oblivious to the erotic meanderings of her wayward thoughts.

She wished! Oh, how she wished!

Her heart was bumping uncomfortably against her ribs—and not just because of the effect Matt was having on her.

Her own honesty compelled her to admit that the attack on her neighbour had shocked and frightened her. She was extremely apprehensive at the thought of spending the night alone, worrying that the attackers might decide to come back!

'I don't have much of an option, do I?' she asked Matt, saccharine-sweetly. 'But I warn you my spare room is very small and has a single bed. A very small single bed.'

'I'll live,' Matt answered laconically. 'Give me your keys.'

Idiotically she handed them to him, her heart giving a funny little skip beat at the intimacy such an action suggested. And then it gave a much stronger kick as Matt's hard, warm fingers closed around her own. Inside her head she had a sudden mental image of him enfolding her hand within his own and them sliding his fingers between hers, and inside her body she had an immediate and explicit surge of aching heat.

Hot-faced, she dragged away her hand and then berated herself mentally for being so vulnerable and weak-willed as Matt let them both into her small, cosy home.

And Harriet's home *was* cosy. As cosy as a small, neat and warm little nest. Her little front room was painted cream, to match the cream rugs on the polished floorboards, and Harriet had made the curtains herself, in a natural woven fabric. Her log-burning stove was her pride and joy, a bargain buy from a scrapyard, and the small terracotta linen-covered sofa had been cadged from her parents and reupholstered for her as a moving-in present.

Harriet could see Matt staring around the small room before following her into the kitchen, with its dining area in the conservatory addition.

Harriet had painted the cheap flat pack kitchen units herself, after bullying Ben to help her assemble them, while her dining room furniture had been junk shop finds which she had patiently restored.

As he looked around the comfortable kitchen, with its cream painted units and earthy-toned décor, Matt acknowledged that it took far more than an expensive designer to create a home—and, moreover, whatever it did take Harriet had it in spades.

To Harriet, though, his silent inspection of her small home spoke of arrogance and even possibly contempt. After all, she had heard all about Matt's state-of-the-art expensive penthouse from Ben.

'You don't have to stay here,' she told him fiercely. 'It was your choice. Not mine. My home may not compare with yours—'

'No, it doesn't.' Matt stopped her grimly.

His rudeness momentarily silenced her.

What would Harriet say if he told her how much he had grown to detest the sterile bleakness of a place that not even the most charitable person could call a home?

Broodingly he roved around the kitchen whilst Harriet watched him resentfully. What was he doing? Trying to make the point that her small home made him feel confined?

'Look, there's really no need for you to stay here,' she said. 'I can always ring Ben and ask him to come over.'

Immediately Matt swung around. 'Oh, yes, you'd like to do that, wouldn't you? Like hell you will, though! Hasn't anything I've said to you sunk in? The whole purpose of this…this…'

'Farce?' Harriet supplied bitterly for him.

'This exercise,' Matt continued, ignoring her, 'is to put a barrier between you and Ben, not give you the excuse to invite him to share your bed!'

'He would not be sharing my bed!' Harriet protested, rushing into impetuous denial. 'When he stays here he always sleeps in his own room.'

'His own room?'

Harriet could understand the hard edge to Matt's voice, but not the white line of tightly reined in emotion around his mouth.

'I suppose you even sleep in the damn bed after he has gone, do you? Dreaming virginal dreams of sharing it with him?'

Now it was Harriet's skin that blanched as fury and shock poured through her in a thunderous fall of ice-cold disbelief.

Turning on her heel, she headed for the door. But Matt got there before her, barring her way with the arm he stretched across it. He felt as shocked by what he had said as Harriet looked, but it was impossible for him to recall the words now.

'Harriet, I'm sorry,' he apologised gruffly. 'I...I was out of order. I shouldn't have...'

Harriet wasn't sure she could trust herself to speak, so instead she put both her hands on his arm and pushed hard against it, to make him remove it from the doorway and let her walk away.

Which was a mistake.

A big mistake. As she discovered when, instead of giving way, his arm pushed hers back and then snapped around her along with its fellow, so that she was tightly bound against Matt's chest.

'Let go of me!'

Not only was her demand ineffectual, it was also muffled against Matt's body, Harriet recognised weakly.

'Not until you've let me apologise!'

Was he serious? Did he realise just how many apologies he now owed her?

'For what?' she asked him pithily, if somewhat breathlessly, and she tussled to put enough space between his flesh and her lips so that her own breath didn't come bouncing back to her off his skin and, by some alchemic means, taste of him! 'Insulting me or imprisoning me?'

'I shouldn't have made that comment about your virginity.'

Harriet went completely still, and then took a deep, shuddering breath.

As though he knew she was going to try and lie to him, Matt added quietly, 'Ben told me.'

'Ben?'

'He thought it was something I should know... Just in case my intentions towards you weren't serious. He may not love you as you want him to, but it's obvious that he feels a...a certain sense of...of responsibility towards you.'

Matt discovered that he was having to battle with himself to make that admission. It would have suited his purpose far better had he been able to point out to Harriet that Ben had no feelings for her of any kind.

But Harriet was barely aware of the last part of his speech. All her concentration was focused on those three appalling words—*Ben told me.*

Never had Harriet wished more that she were the fainting type. Deprived of the opportunity for such an escape, she contemplated the effectiveness of a long, piercing scream—but abandoned it as pointless.

Instead she took a deep breath and said heavily,

carefully spacing out each word, 'Ben told you that I am a virgin?'

Did she realise how cute she looked, breathing heavily down her nose like that when she was angry? Matt wondered adoringly.

'He was trying to protect you!' Matt found himself defending Ben in a gesture of male solidarity, but then he saw the smouldering volcano of wrath that was burning in her furious gaze.

'Oh, yes, I'm sure he was,' Harriet burst out furiously. 'After all, he's been doing it ever since I hit puberty, when he told me that boys only wanted one thing! What is it about you men?' she demanded in a wearily aggrieved voice. 'Ben would run a mile if he found out that a girl he was dating was a virgin, but he expects me to…to feel grateful to him for preserving mine when… Oh, this is just too much!' she exclaimed. 'How could he do this to me? Doesn't he realise that if you and I were in lo— Er, I mean, if we were seeing one another you would have discovered for yourself long before now that I hadn't slept with anyone before?'

Discovered for himself? Long before now? Matt found that he was suddenly having a great deal of trouble breathing. To calm himself down he forced himself to play devil's advocate. 'Perhaps I'm so passionately in love with you that I'm prepared to wait?'

Harriet gave him a narrow-eyed look of open female contempt.

'Because I want to make our first time extra special for both of us…' he elaborated.

Hell, what was he saying that for? Matt cursed as his own body reacted immediately and openly to the intimate images his words were conjuring up.

Harriet could feel herself starting to tremble. No, not tremble. It was a small, delicious, erotic shudder of anticipatory pleasure that was galvanising her body, making her feel so sensuously boneless and weak that she couldn't move a single muscle to prise her eager flesh away from the hardness of Matt's body.

The hardness! Matt had an erection, and her body was savouring that knowledge as her hips ground hungrily against him.

A man could drown in the deep green pools of Harriet's gaze, Matt decided rawly, as his hands slid lower to lift her more tightly against him. His own gaze lowered from her eyes to her mouth, and all hell broke loose inside him.

Inside him—and somewhere upstairs inside the house, where the crash of splintering glass shocked through the silence.

'Wait here,' Matt commanded as he released her, but Harriet ignored him, following him as he took her stairs two at a time and then almost cannoning into him as he threw open the door to the small bedroom which overlooked the street. Harriet paled as she saw the broken window and the glass covering the bed and the floor.

Amongst the glass was a brick. Matt frowned and said, 'Ten to one this is the work of those louts who attacked your neighbour. There's no point in ringing the police at this time of night—we'll do that in the morning. You'd better pack a case.'

'What?' Harriet shook her head vehemently. 'Nothing is going to make me leave here. They might come back, and if the house is empty...'

'Nothing?' Matt queried meaningfully.

Harriet frowned in confusion, not following his train of thought.

She could see the impatient rise and fall of his chest as he breathed in and then exhaled.

'No way am I leaving you here on your own. The other bed is covered with shards of glass which means that if you opt to stay here then I shall be sharing your bed!'

Harriet dropped her gaze hurriedly. Ben was always telling her that she had give-away eyes, and she did not want Matt to see the little gleam in them that said her body was reacting to his threat more as though it had been a promise!

Of course it would be impossible for him to sleep on her small sofa; it was too small even for her!

'Don't worry, you and your virginity will be perfectly safe.' Matt deliberately injected an urbane, almost bored note into his voice.

Harriet swallowed hard on the small lump of disappointment clogging her throat. 'But you said that if…' Self-consciously she fell silent, leaving Matt to agree laconically.

'If I was passionately in love with you it would be different. Yes…' As Harriet turned away from him, intending to go and get something to clear up the mess, he added sardonically, 'I suppose you have some crazy idea of saving yourself for Ben?'

Harriet was too outraged to be cautious.

Turning around, she told him explosively, 'Absolutely not! I haven't any intention of saving myself for anyone! There are two reasons why I am still a virgin. One of them is Ben's wretched dogged persistence in behaving like a moralising big brother whenever any man gets near me. And the other is—'

'Yes?' Matt prodded politely 'The other is...?'

Unable to look at him, Harriet muttered, 'The other is that as yet I haven't found anyone I want...that is, someone who I... Oh, for goodness' sake,' she said in exasperation. 'None of this is any business of yours. Have I quizzed you about your virginity?'

Matt started to shake with laughter. For some reason her angry and grudging admission had made him feel extremely light-hearted. 'No, but since you have now raised the subject I am quite happy to tell you that I lost it on my eighteenth birthday to an older woman—she was all of twenty-one, and in the throes of a break up with her partner. Somehow I don't think I created a very good impression!' he added drily.

Not then, perhaps, Harriet reflected achingly, but since then she had no doubts whatsoever that there were any number of women who had some very special sensual memories of what it was like to share Matt's bed.

As she walked away Matt had to give his libido a severe talking to.

'Well, I think that's the worst of the glass cleared up, and that cardboard I've put over the window should hold up until the glazier gets here.'

Matt stretched and yawned whilst Harriet watched with a fixed, strained expression on her face.

It had taken Ben three months to assemble her kitchen units and put them in place. Three months of spending hours on end in the confinement of her kitchen with him, breathing in the air of his exertions, and yet not once, not one single time, had she felt as she did right now with the scent of Matt's working male body filling the space around her and her body reacting it as though to some kind of nuclear sexual turn-on. Bottle it and women would be aching with lust twenty-four hours a day. She certainly had been ever since she had met him!

'A king-size bed?'

Matt had not added the words 'for a virgin' but he might as well have done, Harriet thought as he came to an abrupt halt just inside the door of her bedroom.

'It was a present from my brother and my sister-in-law,' she told him coldly.

'Mmm… Think they might have been trying to tell you something?' Matt asked, quirking one eyebrow.

'Look, there's no need for you to keep harping on about my…about it. I don't know why on earth Ben had to tell you anyway,' Harriet seethed.

'I've already explained. He wanted to make sure I had honourable intentions towards you,' Matt answered her.

'Honourable intentions!'

Harriet's pretty white teeth snapped together in frustration.

Her bedroom echoed the natural colours and fabrics of the rest of the house, Matt recognised when he managed to drag his gaze away from her long enough to glance around it. The room was dominated by the large bed, with its cream throw, and also held a faint but to him very discernible echo of Harriet's scent— her own scent, not the pretty floral perfume she wore for work.

He smothered a small groan! How the hell was he going to sleep, with her lying beside him and the scent of her all around him, when his body ached so damned much for the feel of her, the taste of her, the sweet, erotic moaning cry of her as he…?

He dragged himself from the dangerous scenario he was mentally creating to hear Harriet saying in a businesslike manner, 'I think I've got a spare robe you can use…'

'Spare? You mean Ben's?' Matt challenged her brutally.

Harriet paled, but stood her ground. 'No, I do not mean Ben's. Actually, I bought it for my father to use. He and my mother stayed here and looked after the house for a few days whilst I was away on holiday last year.'

'Ah…'

Matt was tempted to apologise, to tell her that he was only goading her for her own good, so that she would realise the folly of clinging to an outworn fantasy of having a relationship with Ben and see for herself how much more she would enjoy having one with him!

But Harriet had her back to him and was pulling open a drawer to rummage inside it, muttering, 'It's in here somewhere…'

Matt held his breath as a small scrap of silk and lace fell on the floor. A cream silk thong? With ribbon ties? His imagination was running riot and so was his arousal level. One tug of his teeth and those bows would be history! They would be history, but the soft female flesh they concealed would be his!

As she found the robe Harriet gave a sigh of relief and closed the drawer, only seeing the thong as she did so.

She was closer to it but Matt was faster, and to her

outrage he dangled the small item of underwear from one finger in front of her.

'A present?' he said provocatively.

'Certainly not,' she told him primly. 'I bought it myself!'

Too late she recognised the trap he had set for her.

'Even virgins like pretty underwear,' she said crossly, pink-cheeked.

'This is not pretty underwear,' Matt informed her immediately. 'This, let me tell you, in every male lexicon there is, is classified as provocative and sexy!'

'Provocative and... Oh...!'

'Bra to match?' Matt questioned interestedly.

Harriet's bosom heaved and jiggled distractingly, causing Matt to pay it more attention than her answer.

Out of nowhere a surge of hot, driving male possessiveness overwhelmed him and he had a primitive urge to lock Harriet and her underwear away where no other man could see them. Preferably in a bedroom... His bedroom...

'Do you want to use the bathroom first?' he heard Harriet asking him frostily.

'First? You mean we aren't going to be using it together?' he joked. 'It's ages since someone scrubbed my back for me!'

Harriet was exhausted. Her hormones didn't know where they were. They knew where they wanted her to be, though. Lying pinned to the bed beneath the hot and aroused weight of Matt's preferably naked body, whilst he...

It was just as well she still had those thermal pyjamas her great aunt had so kindly given her last Christmas. She could just imagine what Matt would have to say about her normal habit of sleeping in the nude!

CHAPTER FOUR

HARRIET huffed as she rolled over and into the bank of spare pillows she had insisted on placing down the middle of the bed between Matt and herself—after Matt had announced his intention of sleeping in the nude and had refused to change his mind.

'It's the way I always sleep,' he had told her dismissively.

It was also the way she always slept—but not on this occasion.

'Anyway, you're wearing enough for both of us,' he had added drily.

Harriet made a small sound of irritation as she tried to pull the itchy fabric away from her skin. She was too hot...too wide awake...and much, much too conscious of the man lying peacefully asleep in the bed beside her. Not that she could see him, with the pillows in between them, but if she pushed one of them down a little bit...

Matt was lying with his back to her, his dark head a blur on the white pillow, his bare arm thrown over the duvet, the rest of his body outlined beneath it.

Harriet made a small frustrated sound beneath her breath, released the pillow and rolled over onto her stomach.

But the damage was done and the mental image stored inside her head would not go away.

The trouble was that she was used to having the

whole of the large bed to herself to stretch out in, instead of being hedged in with pillows; that was what was keeping her awake! But Matt was fast asleep, so there was really no harm in removing the pillow barrier now, was there?

Stealthily Harriet removed the pillows and dropped them onto the floor at her own side of the bed.

Cautiously opening one eye, Matt watched her, hastily feigning sleep when she turned back towards him.

Now that Harriet had removed the barrier, nature could do the rest, he decided happily, and he rolled a little closer to the centre of the bed and felt it depress beneath his weight.

Bemusedly Harriet felt her body start to move…as though she were lying on a slope, she decided vaguely. Not that it mattered. Not really. Matt was fast asleep, after all, and she was wearing her pyjamas.

Matt wasn't wearing anything, though. And now he had turned around in his sleep. To Harriet's mortification, as she rolled into him he threw one bare leg over her and pinned her against the bed.

She tried to move, discreetly and silently, so as not to wake him, but for some reason the more she tried to ease herself away the heavier and more imprisoning the weight of his leg became.

Despairingly, she contemplated physically pushing him away, but just as she was about to touch him he muttered something in his sleep and she froze, alarmed that he might wake up.

Instead he muttered again, then lifted his arm and wrapped it around her.

She was trapped in the bed, imprisoned against him

and unable to do a single thing about it without waking him.

And she didn't want to do that!

So she might just as well succumb, then, mightn't she?

A fierce shudder of pleasure ran through her at the mere thought of sleeping wrapped in Matt's arms, her body pressed against the hot satin warmth of his skin.

If only she wasn't wearing Great-Aunt Madge's wretched pyjamas!

If only she might have the courage to reach out and make a leisurely exploration of the sensual feast of naked Matt now so temptingly within her reach.

It would be a crime to waste such an opportunity—especially when she had dreamed wantonly of it and of him virtually from the first night she had met him!

Unfortunately the fact that she couldn't move her arms without risking disturbing Matt meant that she had to be inventive in the way she indulged herself in her voyage of exploration. But happily she soon discovered that her lips and her tongue were avid and acutely sensitive sensory tools.

For the first time in his whole adult life Matt truly and fully understood the meaning of the phrase 'hoist with his own petard.' His subtle machinations had backfired—explosively—on him! He didn't dare so much as move a muscle. If he did…

A low male groan bubbled in his throat. Harriet wriggled uncomfortably in the itchy fabric of her pyjamas and yawned hugely. The events of the day were catching up on her. She yawned again and nestled closer to Matt, making a soft almost purring noise in the back of her throat.

*   *   *

At some point in the night she half woke up. Bewildered to find she was wrapped in something irritatingly itchy and unwanted, she pulled off her pyjamas and then curled back against Matt with a sigh of relief.

Matt woke up first, registered the soft silkiness of bare skin next to his own, and cursed beneath his breath as his body immediately reacted to it. His movement away from her woke Harriet, who pushed back the bedclothes sleepily.

Unable to stop himself, Matt let his hungry gaze drink in the sight of the soft full globes of her breasts. In the coolness of the morning air her nipples were erect and tipped with rose brown against the paleness of her skin. His hands ached to cup and mould them. When she felt his mouth on them would she arch back in eagerness, to give herself freely to him, her fingers locking in his hair as she urged him to take the tight peaks deeper into his mouth and suckle pleasure from them? Would she part her legs and offer him the soft triangle of curls at the apex of her thighs, urging him to stroke the mounded flesh they covered and then move lower, parting the neatly folded lips, sliding between them, slipping between them as her body swelled and moistened for him?

What the hell was he trying to do to himself? His erection was already so damned hard he didn't dare move.

'What have you done with my pyjamas?' Harriet demanded wrathfully as she grabbed the duvet and hauled it up to her chin.

'I haven't done anything with them!' Matt denied. 'You were the one who removed them!'

'What? No, I didn't,' Harriet protested hotly. 'I

would never—' Abruptly she stopped suddenly as she had an unwanted flash of memory of itchy fabric and her desire to be rid of it.

'Harry, is that Matt's car outside—? Oh, whoops!'

They had both been so engrossed that neither of them had realised there had been a brief knock and the bedroom door had been pushed open by Ben!

As she saw him Harriet gave a small squeak and dived beneath the duvet, leaving Ben to go slightly red and look a little bit sheepish.

Matt said calmly, but with an unmistakable edge to his voice, 'Yes, it is my car, Ben. How did you get in, by the way?'

'I've got a key,' Ben told him easily, making a swift recovery as he responded to Matt's calmness, adding hopefully, 'I just thought I'd call 'round and see if I could use Harry's washing machine. Mine's broken, and I didn't fancy the laundrette.'

'Tell him he can use the machine, but I am not doing his ironing,' Harriet muttered from beneath the duvet.

'I've got a better idea, Ben,' Matt announced crisply. 'Why don't you go and buy yourself a new washing machine—you can send me the bill. And I will change Harriet's locks. In fact, if you give me a minute I'll come down with you now, see you out and relieve you of your key.'

Pleasant though Matt's voice was, Harriet could hear the steel in it.

The moment the two men had gone she escaped from the bed and grabbed her robe, pulling it on and making a dash for the bathroom.

When she had showered and dressed behind the safety of the locked door Matt still hadn't returned. It occurred to her that he might not be going to, that he might simply have decided that it would be easier and more tactful for him to leave without saying a formal goodbye!

It was certainly a sensible means of bringing to an end an episode which she suspected neither of them would want to dwell on—although for very different reasons.

Sensible or not, though, it was certainly having an irritatingly irrational and unwanted lowering effect on her spirits, Harriet admitted, as she tugged a brush ruthlessly through her hair and reminded herself that she had far more important things to do than languish about aching for a man who didn't want her.

There was the broken window to report, for a start, and then the glass to get fixed. A small shiver ran through her at the thought of her own vulnerability.

Taking a deep breath, she reminded herself that she was a modern, independent woman and that it was ridiculous of her to feel sorry for herself just because Matt wasn't here to share such tedious practical chores with her.

Opening the bedroom door, she stepped through it and came to an abrupt halt, her eyes widening in disbelief as her gaze swivelled to the bed, where Matt was lying propped up against a bank of pillows—the same pillows she had thrown out last night. He was wearing the robe she had bought for her father, and it was so loosely tied that it was gaping open to reveal an erotic baring of body hair. She ached to ruffle it with her fingertips and...

Hastily Harriet grabbed hold of her rebellious and far too dangerous thoughts, focusing instead on the wrath-provoking fact that Matt was not just lying back at ease on her bed but was also reading her paper, whilst next to him on the bed was a tray of tea and a plate of hot buttered toast. As she sniffed its warm, mouthwatering aroma Matt looked up from *her* paper to look briefly at her before raising one eyebrow.

'Why the rush to get dressed?'

'Why?' Harriet gave him an incredulous look. 'In case you've forgotten, Ben just walked in here and found us in bed together!'

Matt started to frown and put down the paper. 'So how is getting dressed now going to affect that? Ben knows that we're a couple.'

Just hearing Matt say in that firm, totally male voice the word 'couple'—as matter-of-factly as though it were the truth—was having the most disturbing effect on her. But it wasn't just Matt's voice that was making her yearn for his calm assertion to be the truth was it?

It *wasn't* the truth! And she needed to get a grip before she became totally lost in a fantasy that could only cause her heartache and anguish, Harriet told herself fiercely.

'What Ben knows is what you want him to know,' she told Matt fiercely. 'What I know is that this whole…mess has been created and caused by you because you will not accept that I have no romantic interest whatsoever in Ben.'

'If I don't believe it it's because your own actions have made it obvious how you feel. And I'm not the only person to see that.'

'If you're talking about Cindi again—' Harriet exploded.

'Yes?' Matt invited her in a dangerous voice. 'What is it with you?' he demanded harshly when Harriet made no response, throwing aside the paper. 'Have you no pride, no self-respect? What will it take to make you recognise what you are doing to yourself?'

'Not you!' Harriet shot back at him furiously.

'If that's a challenge then let me tell you that I'm a man who never ever backs down from one,' Matt warned her softly.

There was a look in his eyes that was mesmerising her, Harriet decided. And a tightening spiral of mingled apprehension and female curiosity exploded inside her at the hint of dark warning in his voice.

Changing tack, she told him recklessly, 'You had no right to make Ben give you his key!'

Matt's mouth tightened, giving Harriet an opportunity to be both bemused and caught off guard by her own immediate desire to find out just how long it might take for someone to kiss the hardness out of his mouth and feel it soften to hungry passion. A small shudder ran through her at the thought of conducting such an experiment herself.

The effect her own thoughts was having on her was distracting her so much that she only just managed to hear Matt's crisp reply.

'On the contrary, I have every right not to want another man to have access to your home, your bed, and most especially to you.'

A weakening female longing ran through her. If only those words were true! And thank heaven that she was not foolish enough to voice that wish!

'The only thing Ben wanted access to was to my washing machine,' she pointed out waspishly, adding, when Matt remained unmoved, 'You do realise that he's now going to think we really are lovers, and that we're…?'

'That we're what?'

'Ben knows I wouldn't go to bed with someone if I didn't…if I wasn't…'

Harriet compressed her lips. 'I think I should warn you that Ben has some pretty old-fashioned ideas about how…well, certain things. And now that he's seen us like this he's going to start asking all sorts of questions.'

'He already has,' Matt informed her nonchalantly. 'Which is why I've told him that we're getting married!'

Getting married!

Harriet couldn't believe her ears!

'Try to look on the bright side,' Matt encouraged her.

'What bright side?' Harriet croaked acerbically. 'How can there be a *bright side?*'

'Well, for one thing Ben isn't going to find it necessary to protect your virginity anymore, is he?'

'But I'm…' Harriet began, and then stopped, colour flooding her face as something in the way Matt was watching her made her heart start to race bumpily. 'This whole thing is crazy. I'm going downstairs to ring the police and a glazier,' she told him crossly.

'It wouldn't have worked, you know,' Matt said as she reached the door.

'What wouldn't have worked?' Harriet demanded.

'Saving yourself for Ben.'

Harriet had had enough. With her hand on the door she told him angrily, 'You are the one who came up with that scenario—not me! So far as I'm concerned my virginity is just an…an unwanted encumbrance, and personally I'd be only too happy to be rid of it. But of course there's no way you are going to believe that, is there? Because there's no way you would ever admit you are in the wrong! You just aren't going to believe it—whatever I say—or do! Not even if I went out and…and…and slept with the first man I could find!'

'Why go *out* to find one?'

Harriet's eyes rounded and she stared at him, not sure if she had misheard or misinterpreted his soft question.

'You mean, I should…you would…?' She stopped and shook her head as her voice became a small, breathless squeak.

Matt gave her a mocking look. 'See what happens when you make theatrical threats you can't carry through?' he taunted her.

'It wasn't a threat—' Harriet started to defend herself, but to her relief Matt's mobile phone started to ring, and as he reached out to answer it she made a swift exit from the bedroom.

Downstairs in the kitchen, as she waited for the kettle to boil, she closed her eyes and leaned against one of the kitchen units.

What if she had taken Matt up on his challenge? What if she had boldly told him that she wanted him to relieve her of her burdensome virginity? What if…?

But she knew that her feelings for Matt would never be satisfied by a clinical cold sex session, no matter how proficiently executed on Matt's part. And, worse than that, she knew that such an event could and would only leave her craving what she had been denied.

Instead of indulging herself in imagining them making love, what she really ought to be doing was worrying about the complications Matt had caused by pretending to Ben that they were getting married.

*   *   *

Matt's telephone call was from Ben, who wanted to tell him how much his washing machine was going to cost.

'Have you and Harry set a date for the big day yet, then?' Ben asked, once Matt had assured him that he meant what he had said about paying for the washing machine.

'We're working on it,' Matt answered, tongue in cheek.

After he had ended the call Matt started to frown. Did Harriet really think he had been deceived by her denial that she wasn't saving herself for Ben?

And as for that idiotic claim she had made—hadn't it occurred to her that he could have chosen to take her words at face value and put her in a position where…?

Where what? Where he would physically take her in his arms and then take her to bed and show her, share with her, so much pleasure that she would never want him to let her go? Where she would love him as he longed for her to do? As though he was the only man she ever could or would love, now and forever!

Matt's frown deepened. The intensity of the feelings she aroused in him still had the power to shock him.

Pushing aside his pain, Matt got off the bed and headed for the bathroom. Did Harriet not realise the risk she had taken? Didn't it occur to her how another man might react to the kind of challenge she had given him? He was beginning to think that for her own protection, and his sanity, he ought not to let her out of his sight!

CHAPTER FIVE

HARRIET had just finished speaking to the hospital to check on her elderly neighbour when Matt walked into the kitchen, and her concern for the old lady was in her eyes as she turned to him and said worriedly, 'Mrs Simmonds's injuries are more serious than they thought. She's fractured her hip and she's still in shock. The hospital says that it could be several weeks before she's well enough to come home. What kind of people would do a thing like that, Matt?' she demanded passionately. 'To a helpless elderly woman…'

'The kind who would do the same thing to a young woman who is equally helpless, even though she might be too damned stubborn to accept that!' Matt warned her grimly.

Harriet gave a little shudder.

'I'm going to ring the police to report the damage here last night, get someone 'round here to install a decent security system, and then—'

'You're going home?' Harriet suggested eagerly.

'And then we are going out shopping,' Matt told her with an unkind smile.

'Shopping?' Harriet queried uncertainly.

Matt leaned back against the wall and folded his arms across his chest 'Shopping! As of now, until I deem it safe for you to be here on your own, you and

I will be sharing the same roof. That roof can be this one—although it could be damned uncomfortable with a team of workmen installing a security system—or it can be mine. I don't care. But what I do care about is that when, as it will do, our relationship becomes public knowledge, you are wearing my engagement ring—here.'

As he finished speaking he took hold of her hand and tapped her ring finger meaningfully.

'What on earth for?' Harriet asked, once her body had stopped reacting to his touch and her emotions had stopped rioting at the thought of what it would be like if he really meant it. 'No one gets engaged these days just because they've spent a night together...'

'No, but they do when they're planning to get married.'

'But we aren't!'

'Ben thinks we are,' Matt reminded her. 'And I intend him to go on thinking that! There's no way out, Harriet,' he informed her. 'I'm not letting you off the hook. You need to break out of this addiction you've developed—for your own sake as much as Ben's and Cindi's.'

'I am not addicted to Ben and I am most certainly not letting you buy me an engagement ring!' Harriet protested. 'Wearing it would make a...a travesty of...of...'

'What you mean is that you don't want Ben to see you wearing my ring. Why not? After all, he's already seen you in bed with me—'

'Exactly!' Harriet pounced triumphantly. 'He's seen me in bed with you, so why does he need to see me wearing an engagement ring?'

'*He* doesn't, but I think it would be better for you..and me—if other people did,' Matt replied obliquely.

'If I loved a man I wouldn't care who knew I had spent the night with him,' Harriet told him passionately, even though a small voice inside her reminded her that Ben would certainly mind, and would be all too likely to assume his big brother role and tell Matt so!

'Maybe not. But if he loved you with the same intensity, and if, like me, he was a certain old-fashioned type of male, who wanted to tell the world how he felt about you and how committed he was to you, he might! In fact there's no might about it! He would!'

Harriet opened her mouth and then closed it again, for once lost for any kind of comeback.

If she refused to go along with what Matt was planning, and if Ben then thought that she and Matt had quarrelled and their 'relationship' was over, he'd be fussing over her like a mother hen—just as he always did when he thought she was upset or in trouble. Harriet could well imagine what that would do to his own relationship with Cindi, especially in view of the ultimatum Cindi had already given him.

Sometimes in life a person had to put another person's feelings and needs before their own. This was her time to do that for Ben, Harriet recognised. She had already come between him and Cindi unintentionally; she certainly wasn't going to risk doing so a second time.

And what was an engagement ring anyway? Nothing permanent or legally binding! If by wearing it she could buy Ben and Cindi enough time to patch up their differences and get their relationship on a sound enough footing for Cindi to have complete trust in Ben's love for her, then that was what she was going to have to do! And besides, seeing her wearing Matt's ring should surely also go a long way to making Cindi herself realise that Harriet wasn't romantically interested in Ben.

'So that's the ring sorted out,' she heard Matt declaring. 'Now, you'd better pack enough stuff to last you at least a week—I've decided it'll be much safer for you to stay at my penthouse…'

'Your penthouse! But that's in our office block! I'm not staying there!'

'Of course you are. What better way could there be to reinforce the fact that we are now a couple?'

Wearing Matt's ring was one thing—moving into his apartment was quite definitely another.

Harriet put up the fiercest fight and the best argument she could against them 'living together,' but in the end Matt wore her down by the simple expedient of steamrollering over every single point she made, and she was forced to give in.

Her hands trembled as she packed her things, her nerves jangled by the situation which had gone way beyond her control.

Why on earth couldn't Matt have simply accepted her assurance that she had no romantic interest in Ben? Instead of involving them both in this increasingly complicated and, for her at least, increasingly dangerous situation!

Miserably she acknowledged that his misjudgement of her was going to expose her to far more emotional danger than she felt equipped to handle—and if, as she feared, she fell even more deeply in love with him he would be the one to blame!

Yes, he would be the one to blame. But she would be the one to pay, in sleepless nights and in a heart and body that ached unbearably for him.

Matt broke his concentration on driving to turn his head and glance briefly at Harriet. She had not spoken a single word to him since they had got into his car, but he could almost smell the hot, slow burn of her angry resentment.

'This city is becoming too damned overcrowded,' he commented grimly as the intersection in front of them became gridlocked.

'That's why so many firms are encouraging their staff to work from home,' Harriet replied without thinking, and angry flags of colour flew in her cheeks when she realised that Matt had tricked her into breaking her mental vow to keep as much distance between them as she could by not talking to him.

'Well, it's an excellent option for some businesses,' he agreed.

'Including yours?' Harriet asked him.

'Maybe in time. I can certainly see that if I were to marry and have children then there would be a distinct appeal in it for me personally. With modern technology I could work from home myself quite easily, and therefore no doubt so too could my employees.'

The very sound of the word 'children' on his lips made Harriet's whole body ache. For them—for him—for the feel of him within her whilst his body and hers created the new life that would be their child.

The feeling that suddenly shook her was like nothing she had ever felt before—immediate, primitive, and possessive of her mate, of their child...of their love.

Unable to bear the intensity of her own emotions, she looked out of the car window and then frowned.

'Matt, where are we going? This isn't the way to the office,' she protested sharply.

'We aren't going to the office. We're going shopping. The engagement ring—remember?' Matt answered as he turned into a narrow street that fed into the car park of an exclusive shopping mall built around the city's most prestigious luxury hotel.

'We'll get the ring and then we'll have dinner here later, to celebrate.'

'Dinner here? We can't!' Harriet panicked. 'I'm not wearing the right clothes.'

Honesty almost compelled her to add that she did not even possess anything remotely suitable to wear at such an exclusive establishment, but before she could do so Matt was shaking his head, telling her, 'Don't worry. I'd like to change, too. I'll book a room and we can shower and change there before dinner.'

When he saw her expression he told her suavely, 'It will be expected. People are bound to ask questions. It would be a very unusual couple who did not celebrate their engagement.'

'We are a very unusual couple,' Harriet reminded him through gritted teeth. But Matt was already pulling into one of the exclusive spaces reserved for hotel guests and the car door was being opened for her, making it impossible for her to continue her argument.

'I've booked a table for dinner and a room,' Matt

told Harriet carelessly ten minutes later, when he returned to her side in the elegant reception area.

'I can't believe you're making all this unnecessary fuss,' Harriet protested.

'If we were really getting engaged would you consider it an unnecessary fuss?' Matt asked her evenly.

'Of course not,' Harriet denied promptly. 'Every woman wants such a special occasion to be…special. Oh!' She gave Matt a glare of goaded anger in response to his infuriating expression. 'If I was really making that kind of commitment, a public dinner in an expensive hotel wouldn't be the way I would want to celebrate it,' she continued passionately.

'No? Then where would you want to celebrate it?' Matt asked her drily.

Looking away from him, Harriet said softly, 'Somewhere private, romantic…and special…where we could be alone.'

'Such as? A silken tent on desert sands?' Matt mocked her, watching her face as she shook her head.

Her eyes were brilliant with emotion, and behind the anger she was showing him the wildly passionate side of her character. There was a longing that softened her mouth and burned hotly in her eyes, and immediately his own body responded physically to it. So much so, in fact, that he had to turn slightly away from her and try to distract her.

'A remote cottage with open fires and soft rugs, perhaps?' he suggested softly. 'Where your lover could lay you down and cover your nakedness with his own whilst he watched the pleasure he was feeling reflect back to him from your eyes?'

As he spoke Matt's voice had deepened and developed a raw note to it that raised the tiny hairs on

Harriet's arms. Deep inside her she felt a piercingly sharp ache.

'Or perhaps you'd like to lie back in a bath scented with rose petals whilst he slowly...?'

Any one of them, Harriet wanted to beg him frantically. Any or all of them—and now, right now...

He was doing it again, Matt warned himself. He was building images, emotions, dreams for himself which had no substance in reality.

But what if...?

What if nothing. He stopped himself sharply.

A little ruefully Harriet acknowledged that a pair of jeans, a tee shirt and a casual lightweight jacket, no matter how much the modern, acceptable and go-anywhere uniform they normally were, were hardly the kind of clothes she would have chosen to wear for an outing such as this one.

No! Had she and Matt really been going to choose her engagement ring, and then going on to celebrate their engagement, she would have wanted to be wearing...

Unbidden, an image appeared inside her head of the bow-tied briefs she had last seen dangling from Matt's fingers. As it just so happened the briefs were part of a matching set, and the bra that went with them tied provocatively at the front with satin ribbons...

Knowing they were going out on such a romantic and emotional mission, wouldn't she have wanted to dress in something suitably reflecting the day's mood and the reason for it?

But if Matt had been watching her dressing...watching whilst she tied those fragile bows...

would they have got as far as leaving their bed, never mind their home?

The images that her over-excited mind were conjuring up brought a feverish flush to her face, and a shallow race to her heartbeat.

As Matt headed for the main exit from the hotel, Harriett discovered that she couldn't resist continuing with her private fantasy. Mentally she covered her breasts and the hard peaking of her nipples against the semi-transparent silk of her bra with a soft cashmere top. Cashmere always felt so sensuous to touch, and, if it was fine enough, when he looked at her Matt would be able to imagine the shape of her breasts, the way he had caressed them during their early-morning lovemaking.

Locked in a battle with her own recklessly wanton imaginings, Harriet froze as Matt suddenly reached out and took hold of her hand, lacing his fingers through hers, and then locking his grip on her when she tried to pull away.

'We're madly in love,' he told her when she gave him a mutinous look. 'Remember?'

'We're in the middle of a shopping mall,' Harriet protested. 'People don't—'

'No?' Matt stopped her. 'Look over there.'

Several yards away from them a couple were walking hand in hand together, obviously completely absorbed in one another. And not a particularly young couple either, Harriet noticed ruefully, as they stopped walking and the man bent to whisper something in the woman's ear. Immediately she turned a radiant face towards him and he moved closer, kissing her tenderly.

For some reason the small intimate scene made Harriet's eyes sting with tears.

'That's different,' she said to Matt fiercely. 'Anyone can see that they really do love one another.'

'You mean because he did this?' Matt challenged softly. And as Harriet turned automatically towards him he reached out with his free hand to cup her face, smoothing her skin with what had to be mock tender fingertips. Harriet could feel the warmth of his breath against her hair, the hard, sure maleness of his hand on her skin. A pulse was jumping frantically at the base of her throat, and her heart was racing to try and catch up with it.

No amount of will-power could stop her from turning her head towards him, green eyes clashing with molten grey. Harriet breathed in sharply and then exhaled on a jagged breath that parted her lips. She could almost feel the molten burn of Matt's gaze on her mouth as he slowly bent his head.

Silently they looked at one another. Her mouth had gone dry, and try as she might she could not drag her gaze away. A sensuous shudder shook her body, and as though it was the signal he had been waiting for Matt covered her mouth with his own.

Was she really making that small, almost incoherent sound of aching pleasure? Was she really turning into the curve of his arm, his body, virtually encouraging him to tighten the intimacy of his hold on her? Shockingly, the mere touch of his lips suddenly became a hard and demanding pressure, and the kiss of passion suddenly overtook convention as his feelings overwhelmed him. As hers were overwhelming her, Harriett admitted dizzily as she returned the hungry pressure of his mouth and longed for the stabbing thrust of his tongue against her own. She wanted to stay like this forever, to feel like this forever. She wanted…

Harriet moaned a small feline protest as Matt softened the kiss and released her mouth.

Reluctantly she opened her eyes and realised where she was and what she was doing.

Wordlessly she looked away from Matt, fighting back over-emotional tears.

Starkly Matt looked at her averted face. Who had she been thinking of when she had returned his kiss with such fierce passion?

Did he really need to ask himself that question? he derided himself bitterly.

Grimly he tightened his grip on her hand, and then inclined his head in the direction of a small coffee-shop. 'Would you like a coffee?'

'What I'd like—' Harriet began through gritted teeth, and then stopped as the outfit displayed in a nearby shop window caught her eye.

A pretty dress, soft and floaty, in delicately patterned silk, it was so beautiful it made her catch her breath. It shrieked that special brand of expensive simplicity and it was just the exact shade of cream that suited her to perfection! In fact it embodied everything she had ever craved in a dressy outfit, right down to the delicate shoes teamed with it. She knew without having to go anywhere near the window that it would probably have the kind of price tag that ran into more than she spent on her wardrobe in a whole year. Even so a small yearning sigh escaped her lips as she had a momentary vision of herself wearing it, with Matt looking adoringly and hungrily at her, and…

Matt frowned as he watched her. There was a rapt, dreamy expression on her face as she stared at the dress in a shop several yards away. A fragile, almost flimsy sort of dress, which would float distractingly around those luscious legs of hers.

Matt's gaze became equally absorbed…

'Excuse me—are you going to go into the coffee-shop? Only, if you aren't…'

Harriet went pink as she realised that she and Matt were blocking the entrance to the café.

'I've just remembered there's a good wine bar right 'round the corner. It's almost lunchtime—we'd be better going there and having something to eat.'

Harriet barely had time to blink before she was being whisked around the corner and down another marble floored walkway into a stylish and very busy wine bar, where Matt somehow managed to get them a table.

They had just given their order when Matt suddenly frowned and stood up. 'I forgot. I need to go back to the cash dispenser. You wait here. I won't be a minute.'

The wine bar certainly had a very glitzy clientele, Harriet conceded as she sipped her drink and waited for their food and Matt's return. She didn't normally come into this part of the city, preferring to spend her spare time in its parks and galleries.

Matt was taking rather longer than she had expected, but fortunately so was their food. Typically, as soon as the waiter appeared with their order, she saw Matt shouldering his way through the crowd by the wine bar door.

'Sorry I was so long. There was a queue,' he informed her as he sat down.

CHAPTER SIX

'WE CAN'T go in here!'

Harriet held back as Matt reached out to ring the discreetly placed doorbell.

'Why not?' he demanded. 'It's a jewelers, isn't it?'

'It isn't just a jewellers,' Harriet hissed. 'It's *the* jewellers...' But it was too late; a smartly suited young woman was opening the door for them and they were being ushered inside.

Even the quiet hum of the air-conditioning sounded expensive, Harriet reflected as she breathed in air scented with just a hint of some discreet perfume.

'Good afternoon, sir, madam. How may we help you?'

'We would like an engagement ring,' Matt announced, squeezing Harriet's hand in warning, as though he had anticipated that she might argue with him.

'Ah... If you would care to come this way? We have a private room.'

The private room was bigger than her small living room, Harriet recognised as they were shown into their seats as carefully as though they were made of precious glass.

'Do you have something special in mind?' the assistant asked Harriet.

'Er…no… Just something simple and small,' Harriet replied uncomfortably.

Why on earth had Matt brought her in here? Even the teeniest chip of diamond they sold would cost the earth—she just knew it.

'My fiancée prefers simple designs,' she heard Matt saying suavely to the woman.

'Perhaps a single stone ring, then? I'll bring some to show you.'

When she came back and put down not a tray but a collection of boxes, each holding the kind of solitaire diamond ring that Harriet had only previously seen on the fingers of the mega-rich, she swallowed and blinked—and tried to keep her gaze averted from one particular ring, which glowed and shimmered and whispered a whole host of tempting things to her.

'I…I thought something smaller…' she said, her voice cracking. She looked down at the array in front of her and whispered, 'Something much smaller.'

The sales assistant's smile had started to dim, and Harriet could feel the grimness Matt was exuding.

'I like this one!' he announced peremptorily, his hand moving and unbelievably picking up the very ring Harriet had looked at.

'Ah.' The sales assistant's sigh was pure liquid approval.

Harriet couldn't help but agree as she looked at the oblong stone in its plain setting, so pure and white that the light dancing on it almost hurt her eyes.

'An excellent choice, if I may say so. And a beautiful stone. Perhaps madam would like to try it on? The band is a little on the small side, but naturally it can be sized to fit her.'

Harriet prayed with all her strength that the ring

would be too tight, that Matt would be forced to pick something else more modest—because she knew he wouldn't want to leave the shop without a ring. But, even though she herself would have sworn that the ring would be too small for her, it slipped down her finger and settled there as snugly as though they had been made for one another.

'Perfect.' The sales assistant smiled.

'We'll have it,' Matt announced.

Ten minutes later, after a celebratory glass of champagne, they were leaving the shop—with the ring.

Harriet barely waited for the door to be closed behind them before turning to Matt and bursting out, 'I can't wear that ring!'

'Why not? Because Ben isn't the one who is giving it to you?' Matt shot back brusquely.

'No!' Harriet denied fiercely. 'It has nothing to do with that!'

'Then what has it to do with?' Matt enquired sharply.

'It's far too expensive.'

'Engagement rings are supposed to be expensive.'

'No!' Harriet corrected him emotionally. 'Engagement rings are supposed to be a token of love and commitment. If I ever do wear one, those are the yardsticks I shall measure it by...not...not its financial value. But then it's typical of men like you, Matt, that you should insist on picking something so expensive—a status symbol ring so that everyone can see how rich and powerful you are!'

Harriet knew that part of her furious outburst was fuelled by her own inner cocktail of volatile emotions. After all, she was in a false engagement to the man she had fought so hard to pretend she did not love, only to recognise instead how very, very much she did love him. It was an act which should have been filled with love and joy, but instead it had merely been a cold financial transaction, resulting in a physical ache deep inside, that gnawed unceasingly at her, and a growing resentment at being misjudged and condemned for a non-existent crime. For some reason Matt's purchase of the ring symbolised for her the combined pain of all of those feelings.

Perilously close to tears, she started to walk away, gasping in protest as Matt's hand shot out, his fingers curling around her wrist as he yanked her back towards him.

Her heart hit her ribs in one shocked beat when she saw how anger had turned his skin bone-white around the mouth, and frozen the grey of his eyes to silver.

'No, Harriet, what's typical of a man like me is that when I put my ring on the finger of the woman I love, I want the world to see that love reflected in it. And, more importantly, I want *her* to see that love, to know my love. To know that just as the ring is unique and beautiful, so to me is she. The purity of the stone reflects my belief in the purity of the love we share, untainted and unmarked by any past loves. I want her to see in its strength the strength of my love for her, and in its flashing fire the fierce heat of my passion for her. But more than anything else Harriet, I want her to look at the ring and know that what truly binds us to one another are bonds we ourselves have chosen—bonds that go way above and beyond any mere ring!'

Harriet couldn't bear to speak. She felt as though her emotions had been cut to ribbons and were now so painfully raw that she felt sick with the agony of them.

Knowing that one day Matt would love someone just as he had described to her, and that that woman would not be her, had opened a door for her on a whole new world of pain.

'Change the ring if you wish to do so,' Matt said tersely. 'It really doesn't matter to me.'

But it did matter, he acknowledged inwardly. He had seen how Harriet's gaze had been drawn to it, and crazily he had hoped…

'Let's get out of here,' he said curtly. 'I'll—' He started to frown as his mobile rang, and as she heard him talking Harriet recognised that his caller was one of his main clients.

'I've got to go into the office,' Matt told Harriet crisply when he had finished. 'Jardines need the Mortlake site package we did for them retailored urgently.'

'I'll come with you,' Harriet offered immediately. He frowned again, so she added, 'I worked on the original with Ben and Charlie.'

'Okay… We'll get a taxi—it will be quicker than getting the car,' Matt said, and he hurried her towards the exit.

'How much reworking do we have to do?' Harriet asked as he hailed a cab.

Jardines was a large accountancy firm and Matthew Cole Ltd was designing their new head office.

'Enough!' was Matt's unforthcoming reply as they got in the cab.

'Dammit, this isn't going to work!'

As she heard the frustration in Matt's voice Harriet

got up from her own terminal and walked across to his office and peered over his shoulder at his computer screen.

'Look at this,' Matt told her grimly, drawing her attention to one particular detail. 'Jardines need this aspect, because it's one of their trademark fixtures, but because of the extra meeting rooms they've asked to have included it just isn't going to configure.'

Frowning, Harriet leaned closer, wholly absorbed in the complex problem on the screen. Her hair fell forward as she did so to brush against Matt's hand.

'I can see what you mean,' she agreed, every bit of her attention focused on the screen as she peered at it and then drew back slightly. 'I think—' she began, and then stopped.

'Yes?' Matt encouraged her.

Harriet shook her head. 'I don't know if it will work, but maybe if you moved the main block to here and streamlined the add-ons, then perhaps you could turn the signature piece at an angle...'

'Show me,' Matt commanded, moving back so that she could get closer to the screen.

Matt had already suspected that she was one of the most proficient and innovative lateral thinkers on his team, and now she was proving it to him.

Quickly Harriet slid into the chair he had vacated. She had worked like this with other people a hundred thousand times—two heads close together over the screen, two bodies sharing the same small space meant for one as they worked to resolve a problem— but that kind of proximity had never affected her like this before. Now it breached her professionalism and distracted her from what she was doing, she admitted, as a sharp frisson of hot awareness heightened the effect of the adrenaline already rushing through her veins and her brain worked overtime to solve the problem in front of them.

Working under pressure like this always excited and energised her, and she felt a surge of professional pleasure as she showed Matt what she meant.

Tensely Matt watched her, quickly picking up on what she was trying to do and moving even closer to work with her.

'Yes. Yes! That's it! Harriet, you've done it!' he exclaimed triumphantly. 'And if we take this out of here, and add it on here...'

Harriet's eyes widened appreciatively as Matt took up her thought process and ran with it, refining and honing it with skilled expertise.

'We've got it. Got it!' Matt exulted, standing up and drawing Harriet with him. 'Good thinking, Harriet!' he praised her, and then leaned forward and brushed her cheek with his lips in relieved appreciation.

'I'm glad I was able to help,' Harriet answered, her voice fading away as somehow her gaze became focused on his mouth and her heartbeat started to hammer.

She heard Matt mutter something under his breath, and in the next second she was in his arms, his mouth on hers.

Harriet heard herself moan as her lips parted and his tongue found hers. The high-voltage tension caused by the intensity at which they had been working must have caused Matt's sudden explosion of passion, Harriet decided dizzily, as his tongue plunged deeper and his hands dropped to her hips, pulling her into his body.

Her own body's swift recognition of his erection sent messages to her brain that had her wanting to explore it more intimately, to run her fingers over it, stroke it, savour it, feel the thick, full hardness of it naked beneath her touch.

A violent shudder racked her body and Matt groaned, his fingers kneading the rounded curves of her bottom, urging her even closer to him. The desk was only just behind her, and inside her head feverish images were already forming.

Matt moved his hand, cupping her breast gently, plucking the pouting tightness of her nipple through her top and making her moan eagerly into his kiss.

He pulled her top out of the way, fiercely and urgently, as though he was as out of control as she felt, Harriet recognised weakly when he pushed aside the fabric of her bra and then lowered his mouth to her breast.

A thrill of primitive female pleasure engulfed her as Matt tugged passionately on her nipple. Her hands reached to clasp his head against her body whilst her body arched in immediate eager response.

The office's muted hum was being overwhelmed by the unsteady sound of their ragged breathing and the hard suckle of Matt's mouth on her breast—an erotic overture that heightened Harriet's arousal and totally drowned any inner voice of caution as its siren call dragged her deeper and deeper into her need.

Outside, down below them, an ambulance siren suddenly wailed into clamouring life.

Immediately Matt released her and stepped back from her, his reactions far, far faster than her own. Her body was aching tormentedly, still clamouring for his touch whilst she struggled to make her trembling hands restore order to her clothes.

'Harriet— Believe me, I never intended...' She could hear Matt speaking grimly, his obvious and immediate rejection of what had happened forcing her to follow his example—for the sake of her pride if nothing else.

'I... I...it doesn't matter. There's no need to make an issue of it,' she said quickly, mortified by the thought that he might start to question just why she had responded to him so immediately and so intensely. 'It wasn't important, Matt. Sometimes these things happen when you're working at high pressure.'

To her relief Matt had turned his back to her, and therefore he couldn't see just how much he had actually affected her.

'Do they indeed?' There was an odd inflection in his voice, but before Harriet could question it he was continuing almost brusquely, 'Look, it's gone six o'clock. I'll call you a cab and you can go back to the hotel and get ready for dinner. The table isn't booked until eight. That will give me time to send this stuff off to Jardines, then get changed here and meet you at the hotel.'

'Do we have to have dinner?' Harriet asked him warily.

'It's a damned sight safer option that staying here and finishing what we just started,' Matt answered her brutally. 'And let me warn you that right now, the way I'm feeling, it would be damnably easy to stand in for Ben and play out your little fantasy for you, if that's the way your mind is working.'

'No, it is not!' Harriet denied immediately, but her face was burning. Inside her a voice was urging her to give in to her real feelings and take what he was offering without questioning the reasons for his offer, no matter what the consequences!

For a moment she was almost tempted to tell him that the only man who ever featured in her sexual fantasies was him, but somehow she managed to stop herself.

'I'll call that taxi,' Matt said flatly.

As he walked away from her he was cursing himself under his breath. If he didn't get some space between them, and soon, he would be taking her up to the penthouse with him—if he could last out that far—and the kind of sex they would be sharing would be hot and immediate and dangerously soul-baring.

At least if he sent her straight to the hotel he would be able to calm himself down. A cold shower might be a good idea as well, he derided himself, as he felt the almost painful ache of his straining erection.

What the hell was happening to him? The thought of having sex here in the office would normally have been more of a turn-off for him than a turn on!

He had booked a room, Matt had said, but this wasn't a mere 'room,' it was a palatial suite! Round-eyed, Harriet looked at the table the waiter had just wheeled in and left: mouthwatering-looking canapés, strawberries dipped in chocolate, champagne on ice—a truly romantic offering! Had someone told them they were about to celebrate their 'engagement'?

Just thinking about it sent a surge of stomach churning mixed emotions racing through her. Her heart twisting, and on edge, Harriet walked through the bedroom. The business clothes she had in her case were hardly going to suit the occasion, were they? She hadn't packed her black dress, and—

Abruptly she came to a halt as she stared at the huge bed, and the glossy designer carrier bag on it.

There was a card pinned to the bag with her name on it in Matt's handwriting. Uncertainly she took it off and read it: *Hope I've got the right size.*

Frowning, Harriet withdrew the tissue-wrapped package from the carrier bag and opened it, her heart somersaulting with a mixture of disbelief, angry pride and a sharp pang of pure female delight, which she tried to subdue as she saw the dress she had admired earlier in the day.

What on earth—? How on earth—? It had to be mere chance, didn't it, that Matt had bought her this particular dress? His action had to have been motivated by his desire not to be shown up by her, didn't it?

That knowledge alone should have had her wrapping the dress up immediately and refusing to even look at it, never mind thinking about wearing it! And perhaps if it had been any other dress but this one she would have done just that. But as she shook it free of the tissue Harriet caught her breath. It was so perfect for her, and the right size as well. In other circumstances she would have loved wearing such a dress for her lover. Her lover… For Matt.

Emotion choked her.

She wasn't going to wear it, of course. She couldn't! Not the dress or the little strappy shoes that went with it either.

And yet she was holding it up in front of her, and her heart gave a sharp pang as she recognised that she had been right. The dress was perfect for her.

And perfect for the occasion.

She had never owned a dress like this. Matt had never seen her wearing anything that declared so emphatically that this was a dress a woman wore for herself and for a man... Her man.

Wearing such a dress would be almost a declaration. An invitation. At least it would be for her.

And that would certainly be one way of proving to Matt that he was totally wrong about her feelings for Ben, a small inner voice told her recklessly. There was still a sharp sensual ache deep inside her body, and suddenly it became much fiercer, an ache that included longing and excitement as well as arousal.

She gave a small, reckless toss of her head.

Tonight she and Matt would be celebrating their engagement, and if she chose to take the situation he had created a step further, if she chose to take the fantasy a step further, and celebrate it in the most natural way of all for a woman in love to celebrate that love, then why shouldn't she do so? She was an adult, and answerable only to herself.

And, as today had shown, Matt wasn't immune to her—even if it was only sexual desire that aroused him.

Why shouldn't she claim this night as her own? Why shouldn't she claim Matt as her own, even if it was only for a few hours?

The audacity of her own thoughts shocked and excited her, feeding the everlasting flame of her love. Was it really such a dreadful thing for her to want to be with him in the most intimate way possible, the way nature had ordained for a woman to be with the man she loved? And she did so love Matt!

Harriet drew in a deep sigh and touched the delicate fabric tentatively. She didn't have much time to make up her mind. Matt would be here soon. She looked at the chilling champagne. Her heart was racing, her blood seething through her veins as though it was already filled with champagne bubbles. Perhaps if she were to have one glass—just to calm her nerves a little! It was only champagne after all! Quickly before she could change her mind she reached for one of the bottles and opened it neatly.

Pouring herself a glass, she took it into the bathroom with her, appreciatively admiring the extensive and very expensive range of toiletries. The hotel management were certainly thorough; there was even a sealed pack of condoms tucked discreetly into a basket of other personal requisites.

Half an hour later, she was just finishing her second glass of champagne and studying her reflection in the bedroom mirror, when the suite door opened and Matt strode in.

Her heart rocked on its axis and a rush of love surged through her. He had changed his casual clothes for the formality of a dark suit and a shirt and tie, and Harriet feasted her hungry gaze on him for as long as she dared.

When he saw her, Matt came to an abrupt halt.

'The dress was the right size, then?' he demanded almost brusquely.

'It fits perfectly,' Harriet answered softly. 'But you really shouldn't have bought it for me.'

'Think of it as a bonus,' he answered tensely. 'You deserve one after solving the Jardines problem for me.'

He didn't sound like a man who had just had a problem solved, Harriet decided, her own mood altering to match his when she saw the way he was frowning and felt the coldness emanating from him.

'I opened the champagne,' she said. 'Do you want a glass?'

His frown seemed to deepen.

'You were the one who said we had to behave as though we were genuinely celebrating our engagement,' Harriet reminded him, sensing his disapproval.

'In public,' Matt said harshly, immediately flicking back his cuff to look pointedly at his watch. 'Our table is booked for eight and it's almost that now.'

His hostility was flattening the bubbles of her own earlier excitement threatening to steamroller over the sharp thrill of delicious and wanton anticipation the champagne had nurtured. And not just the champagne, if she were honest. The intimacy they had shared earlier had left her sensually intoxicated and eager to continue from where they had left off, leading her into a dangerous world of fantasy. But Matt, it was plain, had totally dissociated himself from what had happened. She couldn't let go of her own dreams so easily, though. Her love was a fierce power, overwhelming her normal caution.

A small spurt of rebellious recklessness kicked dangerously to life inside her.

Lowering her lashes, she tried to hide what she was feeling, unaware of just how unintentionally seductive she looked as she reminded him, 'We're celebrating our engagement. Surely we're allowed to be a little bit late? After all, it's obvious from the champagne the hotel has left that they expect us to have our own private celebration...'

Matt witnessed her unexpected transformation from

virgin into seductive vamp with a feeling in his gut that made him want to take hold of her and—

'How many glasses of that stuff did you say you've had?' he demanded, striding over and removing the bottle from the ice bucket.

'Only two,' Harriet told him defensively. 'Plus the one I poured for you!'

'Three glasses of champagne on an empty stomach?'

There was a look in his eyes that was irritated and then for a brief moment filled with something else— a hot, hungry maleness which he quickly leashed.

'I ate some of the canapés and chocolate strawberries,' Harriet assured him virtuously. 'You should try one, Matt, they're delicious,' she encouraged, picking one up and offering it to him.

When he shook his head, she held the chocolate-coated fruit to her own lips, licking the chocolate coating off with happy and uncalculated sensuality.

Matt closed his eyes.

He had deliberately delayed getting here, knowing that in his present vulnerable emotional and physical state he just could not trust himself to be alone with her. The last thing he was equipped to cope with was this. A Harriet transformed into the most unbelievably irresistible virgin turned vamp, and having an effect on him that made him want to strip that damnably erotic dress she was wearing from her body, pour what was left of her glass of champagne over her skin and lick it from her whilst it cascaded over her breasts and pooled in the hollow her belly before. And as for those strawberries…

He looked into her face and saw the soft, illuminated look in her eyes, the half-shy, half-bold way she was looking back at him. He took a step towards her. If she thought he was going to let her get away with looking at him like that, tormenting him like that… Any minute now she was going to end up on the bed, and he was—

Grimly he closed his eyes and took a deep breath, like a diver who'd just come up for air. She didn't know what she was doing—and she certainly didn't know how he felt, he reminded himself.

Refusing to look at her, he removed the ring box from his pocket.

'Look, get this damned thing on, and then we're going down to dinner. And you are not having any more champagne.'

Harriet tilted her chin.

'We are getting engaged. You have to put the ring on for me,' she told him, waggling her ring finger.

Three glasses of champagne and she was like this? He felt like a hormonal teenager, recognising for the very first time what the male hunting instinct was all about, Matt recognised grimly.

He was sorely tempted to tell her that if he went near her now he wouldn't be putting the ring on her finger, but taking the dress she was wearing off her body.

If Matt came over to her now, she was going to put her arms around his neck and kiss his mouth as she had been longing to do for what seemed like forever, Harriet decided dizzily, far more intoxicated by his presence than she would have been by any amount of champagne. And then she was going to tell him that there was no way she was going to get engaged to him unless he took her to bed first. And then if that didn't work she was going to—

Her gaze swivelled to the suite door as it suddenly rattled and two waiters came in, plainly not expecting to find them there.

'It's all right—you can take the trolley,' Matt said. 'We were just leaving...'

'But please leave the champagne...' Harriet called out, as Matt took hold of her arm and practically dragged her into the corridor.

Before they reached the lift he pushed the ring onto her finger, and all she could do as he bustled her inside it to join the other silent passengers was give him a reproachful glower.

'Have you ever made love in a lift?' she asked him conversationally, once it had stopped and they had got out.

Matt stared at her. Vintage champagne on an empty stomach was obviously a new experience for her.

'No, I haven't,' he told her tersely.

'Have you ever wished you had, though?' Harriet persisted.

'Not as much as I wish you had stopped at one glass of champagne,' Matt said through gritted teeth, and he almost marched her into the hotel's exclusive restaurant area.

Harriet produced another pout, and then became distracted as she caught sight of herself in the bank of mirrors that decorated the corridor.

'This dress is just so lovely,' she sighed. 'It makes me feel like a different person.'

'It's certainly making you behave like one,' Matt allowed drily. If he was honest, Matt knew that if circumstances had been different her unexpected transformation would have had him not just tenderly amused and protective, but more than ready to play the erotic game she had so innocently started.

The sight of Harriet with her inhibitions and her defences removed was proving to be a very dangerous and powerful aphrodisiac so far as he was concerned.

'We've just become engaged,' Harriet reminded him reprovingly. 'I'm supposed to be in love with you, remember?' She flashed her ring at him. 'And I just want you to know, Mr Cole,' she said breathily, mimicking Marilyn Monroe, 'that you are the sexiest man alive and I'd much rather be upstairs alone in the suite with you than down here in the restaurant.'

'Really? Rather than being with Ben?'

'Who's Ben?' Harriet asked him sweetly.

'I take it you won't be drinking any wine with your meal?' Matt asked Harriet drily as they studied their menus.

'No...I think I'd better stick with the champagne,' Harriet answered innocently, looking up enquiringly when she heard him make a muffled sound.

'Why don't you have another coffee?'

'I've already had three cups,' Harriet reminded Matt solemnly as the waiter lifted the coffee pot.

The restaurant was almost empty, and the bubbles of excitement singing in her veins had become a giddy fluttering of butterflies in her stomach as she contemplated what lay ahead.

In fact she was a little surprised that she hadn't had any second thoughts—or abandoned her reckless decision before she could put it into practice.

The truth was, though, that if anything her determination to return to the suite and somehow, by hook or by crook, ensure that tonight Matt became her lover had grown stronger during the evening rather than weaker.

The effects of the champagne she had drunk earlier might have worn off, but the effects of her love for Matt and the intimacy they had shared had not!

'I think they're waiting for us to leave,' she told Matt, ruefully indicating the hovering waiters.

'Yes. If you're sure you don't want any more coffee I'll take you up to the suite,' Matt accepted curtly.

As he escorted her out of the room Harriet turned towards him and whispered mischievously, 'Thank you for my beautiful ring, darling,' and then reached up and pressed a brief kiss to his mouth.

The minute he had seen her safely inside the suite he was going to leave her there alone, Matt decided grimly. She hadn't had any alcohol to drink over dinner, and surely the effects of that damned champagne should have worn off by now, but she had spent the entire evening openly flirting with him. As the lift doors opened and they stepped together into its empty intimacy he decided that he didn't know which he wanted to do the most—strangle her, or...

When he saw that she was looking at him with liquid-eyed expectant hopefulness, he took a deep breath and told himself that he must be imagining things. He made sure he stood well away from her.

The lift took them to their floor and he waited for her to step out. Harriet turned to him and told him reproachfully, 'You might at least have kissed me, Matt. Every woman has a right to be kissed in a lift once in her life—especially when she has just got engaged...'

Removing the suite key from his pocket, Matt unlocked the door and held it open.

Happily Harriet stepped inside, and turned to smile at him.

'Sleep well,' Matt told her dismissively. 'I'll give you a call in the morning.'

Harriet's eyes widened. 'You're leaving me here on my own?'

Matt could hear the disbelief in her voice. 'I might as well go back to the penthouse.'

'Matt!' she protested, unable to conceal her distress. But it was too late—he was already closing the door.

This couldn't be happening to her! He couldn't have left her! But he had.

Harriet blinked hard, swallowing the taste of her disappointment.

So much for her plans!

Matt reached the lift and pressed the bell.

He had done the right thing. He knew that. If he had stayed he could count on one hand the seconds before he would have had Harriet in his arms, showing her just what effect her behaviour towards him over dinner had had on him, and how dangerous it was to flirt with a man as much as she had flirted with him. Especially when that man was already so damned hungry for her that—

The lift arrived and the doors opened.

Matt got in and pressed the button.

Have you ever made love in a lift? What the hell kind of question was that? He closed his eyes and then opened then again as the lift reached the car park floor.

*   *   *

Disconsolately Harriet removed her precious dress and wandered into the bathroom. The whirlpool bath caught her attention and she heaved a small sigh.

She might as well enjoy some sinful self-indulgence, even if it was not the kind she had longed for.

Turning on the taps, she ran a bath and removed the rest of her clothes.

Matt reached into his pocket for his car keys, frowning as he realised that he had only both suite keys.

Now, why on earth had he done that? Or did he really need to ask himself?

Fate was a funny thing, he decided as he locked the car and started to retrace his steps.

Harriet didn't hear him enter the suite. In fact the first she knew of his presence was when he walked into the bathroom to find her lying back in the whirlpool bath, with only her head above the mass of bubbles which had already spilled over the sides of the tub.

'Matt,' she whispered weakly. 'I don't know what I've done, but I think these bubbles are getting a bit out of control.'

'That's what happens when you play around with things you don't understand,' Matt heard himself answering thickly.

Did she have any idea what she was doing to him? As she tried to sit up foam clung to her skin and then slid from it, revealing the creamy swell of her breasts. 'I can't switch the whirlpool jet thingy off.'

'You'd better get out, then, and let me try.'

'It would be much easier if you got in,' Harriet told him softly. 'And much more fun!'

Matt stared at her, but although she flushed slightly she didn't look away from him.

'You do know what you're saying, don't you?' he demanded, before stressing, 'What you're inviting...?'

Mutely Harriet nodded her head, and then told him brightly, 'The hotel is awfully well-organised, Matt. They even provide condoms.' She stood up in the bath. 'Help me out, please.'

'I thought you wanted me to get in with you?' he reminded her huskily.

Matt closed his eyes, exasperated with himself for his own lack of self-control. What the hell was he doing? But it was too late to back out now. Harriet was looking at him, her eyes glowing and an expression of radiant expectancy on her face.

'Oh, Matt!' she whispered. 'I do want you to make love to me so very, very much. You will, won't you?'

CHAPTER SEVEN

HARRIET gave a small gasp as Matt lifted her body out of the bath. 'Your suit!' she protested. 'You'll be soaked... Mmm.'

If *he* didn't care about his suit, then she wasn't going to worry about it! Not when he was kissing her like this.

He should not be doing this, Matt warned himself. But somewhere deep down inside himself he knew that there was no way he could not. Some foolish, stubborn part of him refused to relinquish its passionate belief that if only he could show Harriet what real love—*his* love—was like, then she would recognise how much she wanted it, and him, and how little she wanted Ben.

Harriet hardly dared allow herself to believe what was happening. To believe that it was Matt who was holding her and kissing her. But her body had no time for such foolish hesitations. Her body was far, far too busy showing its appreciation of the sensual pleasure it was enjoying, and what was more it was demanding that Harriet threw every bit of her emotional and cerebral energy and concentration into actively participating!

And why should she not do so, when it was so very, very much what she wanted?

Eagerly she wrapped her arms around his neck and

pressed her naked body as close to him as she could, returning the hard, demanding pressure of his mouth with a kiss of fevered longing. Delicately she ran the tip of her tongue along the line of his mouth, tracing it, probing its defences. She lifted her breasts and the urgent thrust of her body brought a sensually erotic friction to her nipples with each unchoreographed and instinctive movement it made.

Matt had always prided himself on his self-control, but now he realised that it had never previously been truly tested, that all other sensual intimacies had barely touched the surface of what uncontrollable need actually felt like. The feel of Harriet's tongue tip innocently mimicked and mirrored the most intimate kind of man-to-woman penetration; the hard points of her stiff nipples were hot stabs of pleasure burning against his skin with every writhing movement of her body. These were all guided-missile assaults on a defence mechanism which in the past had known little other than the equivalent of a mild attack with a handheld catapult.

Even the erection he could feel straining against his clothes had an unfamiliar dimension to it—not so much in size, or even intensity, but in something that went way beyond that. A sort of spiritually physical homing need, Matt recognised to his own grim shock.

So this was physical love. This savage, untameable hunger that would break down every barrier between them until they were perfectly united as one. This seeking, aching drive to complete himself within her.

What he felt was both primitive and spiritual. The most basic of man's desires and the most elevated, straining together to form an emotional and physical hunger that held him helpless in its grip.

Harriet could feel how aroused Matt was, and beneath the immediate kick of her sweetly pleasurable excitement she could feel the rhythmic pulse of her body's answering response.

Impatiently she tugged at his shirt, her skin starting to flush with betraying heat.

How long was he going to make her wait?'

Somehow her love-hungry thoughts had become achingly impatient words, whispered against Matt's mouth as she tried to steal the intimate kiss she was longing for.

And when he heard them Matt felt the last of his self-control being dragged away with them. He gripped her bare arms firmly and eased her away from his body, ignoring her small moaned protest. When she tried to reach out to him he tugged her hands down and held them carefully with one of his own, whilst he started to undress himself impatiently with the other.

'Wait…just wait,' he told her thickly, his molten grey gaze holding the dark liquid passion of jade.

When he tugged off his shirt he felt the shudder that jolted her through his own body, like an electric shock. Her already prominent nipples flared into irresistible dark-flushed temptation.

Harriet shuddered again when he looked at them, and somewhere inside his head the need to experience how she would react when he gave in to the craving to have her breasts inside his mouth struck him with such force that he had dropped to one knee and begun lapping at first one and then the other with fierce urgency before he could stop himself.

Her hands trapped behind her back, Matt's tongue laving her exquisitively aroused nipples, Harriet shuddered more under the liquid surges of pleasure that ran through her.

Pulling her hands free of Matt's grip, she started to finish the task he had begun, tugging frantically at fabric and fastenings until she could feel the heat of his flesh beneath her hands.

The tug of his mouth on her breast drew a sharp, wild cry from her lips and she raked his flesh with her nails, unable to stop herself from reacting to the needs he was feeling.

She could feel it gathering swiftly inside her, like a fast-flooding river, channelled into the place where its intensity would set in motion a cataclysmically powerful reaction.

Fear spiked and shook her; the swift race might prove too fast to be properly harnessed. As though he sensed it too, Matt swept her up into his arms, kicking aside the tangle of his clothes, and carried her into the bedroom.

In its shadows Harriet could almost see the beat of his heart beneath the golden sheen of his skin. Wonderingly she raised her hand to it, her fingertips measuring each thudding, driving beat, knowing already with the most intense emotion and physical anticipation that soon that driving power would be replicated and intensified within her own body.

Matt could feel the strain on his own self-control as he placed Harriet on the bed. Things had gone too fast, and for him too far now, for the slow, gentle voyage he had intended.

Harriet lay on the bed and looked up at him. She was shockingly close to her orgasm…too close.

In her mind's eye she could see the foil wrapper

of the condom she had secreted away in her handbag, which was within reach beside the bed.

A surge of explicit heat tightened sharply inside her. Deliberately and determinedly she opened her legs, and looked directly into Matt's face.

The dark tide of colour that surged through his face as his arousal strained towards her only heightened her own.

Boldly she touched her own body, biting down hard on her lip as she felt the immediate tense contraction, her gaze fixed fiercely on Matt's as he shuddered violently in response.

'Now, Matt... Oh, please, now—now...' Her words were lost, crushed beneath his mouth as his hands shaped her. She could feel the thick, hard throb of him against her thigh and her fingers reached blindly for him, discarding as they did so the foil wrapper she had been clutching.

Somewhere, outside himself and the ferocity of his driving need, Matt registered and recognised it, automatically responding to his own inbuilt set of unbroken rules.

Harriet, clinging to the edge of a place she couldn't bear to let herself be swept from, heard the brief rustle and felt the chilling emptiness of where he had been. But before she could think logically about what was happening Matt was holding her, kissing her, entering her as slowly and carefully as he could whilst his whole body shook under the unbearable burden of his own self-control. She exhaled a delicious moan of joyous pleasure as she realised that her fantasies were going to be more than fulfilled.

The brief feeling of pressure, the sudden stilling of Matt's body, were unwanted interruptions and delays.

Instinctively she showed him this, moving fiercely and eagerly against him until he drove deeper and then more deeply still as she clung to him and urged him to take all that she wanted to give him, her body glorying in each new thrust.

Dear heaven, but she felt so good, so perfect, with her flesh enfolding him, holding him, gripping him. She moved deliberately against him, inciting him to plunge deeper.

Harriet could already feel her orgasm overwhelming her—tight, fierce bursts of sensation that echoed the pulse of life itself. She heard Matt shout out in exultation and the intensity increased to a frantic explosion of savagely powerful contractions that were a world away from anything she had previously experienced.

Held fast in Matt's arms, still trembling between each jagged breath, Harriet felt herself fall from the euphoric haven she had been inhabiting through doubt and shock into the cold, unwanted world of reality.

Matt was renowned for his astuteness. How long would it be before he guessed how she felt about him? And when he did what was going to happen?

Harriet suspected she already knew the answer to her own question.

She would suffer the misery and the humiliation of being told that Matt did not want her love—and, worse, she would probably be banished from his life! She couldn't bear to let that happen!

She must not let him guess how she really felt!

His chin resting on the top of Harriet's head, Matt blinked fiercely. No one, nothing, had ever touched his emotions so intensely as what he had just shared with Harriet. It was true that love gave the physical act of intimacy between two people an extra dimension that took it into another world. He felt awed, humbled, fiercely and passionately completed, and equally fiercely and passionately determined that he was never, ever going to let Harriet go.

Surely she must have shared some of those feelings?

All his adult life he had protected his own deepest emotions, but now he knew that he had to tell Harriet how he felt, that he had to beg her if necessary to let him wipe the slate clean so that they could begin again—two people who could together touch immortality through their shared love.

He took a deep breath and began, 'Harriet, why—?'

Immediately Harriet froze. It was happening already, the very thing she had dreaded. Matt was going to ask her why she had responded to him in the way she had, and then he was going to answer his own question by telling her that he knew she was in love with him.

She couldn't let that happen.

'I know what you're going to say, Matt.' She stopped him quickly. 'But you've got it all wrong. The only reason I made… I did what I did was because I couldn't think of any other way of convincing you that, contrary to your constant accusations, I am not saving myself for Ben.'

Her sharp, careless words hit Matt like blows, like acid-tipped arrows to his heart. He went completely still, and then moved away from her so brutally that

Harriet felt as though he had physically pushed
her away.

'Thank goodness you were quick-thinking enough
to remember the condom,' she added chattily. 'It was
a wonderful experience, Matt, and I got so carried
away that I would have forgotten.'

There! That should take care of any thoughts he
had of questioning the intensity of her response,
Harriet decided fiercely.

She waited for Matt to respond, but instead he simply got out of the bed and walked silently into the
bathroom, firmly closing the door.

A pain like no other she had ever experienced filled
her. It was so intense, so immense, that she couldn't
contain it. It felt as though it was weeping from her
heart into her blood, seeping through her pores until
every bit of her was saturated with it.

There was no escape from it and there never would
be, Harriet acknowledged in anguish.

CHAPTER EIGHT

NUMBLY Harriet opened her fist and stared at the ring in the palm of her hand. Unable to bear its brilliance in the face of her own pain, she closed her hand again, so tightly that the stone dug into her skin.

She hadn't seen Matt for over a week. He had left the hotel after they had made love without saying a single word to her, and she had discovered when she had arrived at work in the morning that he had been called away on some urgent business.

She had received a terse text message from him, demanding: 'Wear the ring—I meant what I said'.

And of course she'd had to, for Ben's sake! And now it seemed that everyone knew that she and Matt were supposed to be engaged.

Now at last it was Friday, and she had decided it was the last day of her working life with Matt. If she couldn't endure the pain of her unwanted love when he wasn't there then how on earth was she going to bear it when he was?

The tears threatening to pour from her eyes were as sharply painful as the diamond cutting into her hand.

'Harry—there you are!'

She forced a smile at Ben came bounding up to her. 'How's Cindi?' she asked him.

'She's fine. We're both fine. In fact we're over the

moon,' he confessed happily. 'She's finally accepted that she got it all wrong about you and me, and she's taking me home with her to meet her family at the end of the month. But first we're going to have a couple of days away together, so that I can follow Matt's example and pop the question! I love her so much, Harry, but there's no way I could have accepted her if she hadn't been understanding about you and our friendship.'

Harriet's heart sank further with every word he uttered. Everything Ben was saying confirmed what she herself had feared. She suspected that if she and Matt 'broke up' now, it would do irreparable harm to Ben's romance.

But of course the truth was that she and Matt had nothing together to break up. She meant nothing to him. Nothing at all!

Tears filled her eyes. Frantically she tried to blink them away.

'Harry?' Ben queried, bewildered. 'What is it? What's wrong? I thought you were happy.'

It was more than Harriet's savaged emotions could stand. To her own humiliation and disbelief she discovered that she had stared to cry.

'Thank you, Ben. I will deal with this,' Matt announced from behind them.

Both of them swung around in shock, neither of them having heard him come into the room.

'Oh, Matt. It's you! Good.' Ben looked relieved. 'Well, I'll take myself off and...'

'That won't be necessary,' Matt told him grimly. 'What Harriet and I have to say to one another is going to be said in the privacy of my apartment, and not here in the office!'

So far he hadn't so much as looked at her, never mind addressed her directly, Harriet recognised, torn between a sweet, aching longing, unbearable pain, and total and absolute misery.

He was looking at her now, though, pinning her with that ice-grey look of his whilst he held open the office door and said coldly, 'Harriet?'

Reluctantly she started to walk towards him, preparing her verbal defensive attack as she did so.

And she didn't wait to reach him to launch it. 'There really isn't any point in this Matt,' she began, but to her shock he forestalled her, manacling her wrist with a hard, determined grip.

But it was still his touch, still his flesh on hers, and she was still oh, so achingly vulnerable to that.

Panic engulfed her like the cold, icy waters of a well she had fallen into and couldn't escape from.

'No! Let me go. You know—'

Immediately Matt swung around to face her.

He must have been working hard, she decided, because there was a sharper edge to his jaw, a leanness to his face, and the shadow of something in his eyes that suggested a hard, punishing week without proper meals or sleep.

'I know what? How hot you are in bed?' he taunted her savagely. 'Do you want me to tell Ben that? What we have to say to one another needs to be said in private—unless you want me to go into explicit detail in public,' he told her brutally.

Harriet felt herself sway as her body absorbed the shock of his open threat.

He hadn't had a single second's respite from thinking about her all week—which had defeated the whole purpose of setting up a rigorous diary of appointments to keep him out of the office, Matt acknowledged bitterly.

This morning, knowing he would be seeing her, he had been forced to admit that his need to do so had outstripped his pride by about one thousand to one.

He had even planned during his early-morning drive back how he could use the fake engagement he had created to build a very real intimacy between them—the kind of intimacy which, whilst a form of purgatory for him, would at least give him the opportunity to find some way to win her love.

And then he had walked into the office—his office—to find her with Ben!

Matt didn't know how to contain the savagery of his own pain. He told himself that he wasn't going to say a word to her until they reached the penthouse, but no sooner were they outside the room than he found himself breaking his own rules.

'I don't care what you have to say about it, Harriet, or how much you argue,' he told her harshly, 'our engagement is still very much on, and will remain on.'

'You don't—'

'And what is more,' Matt continued thickly, 'if necessary it will be continued as far as marriage.'

'If necessary? What do you mean, if necessary? How could it be necessary? I—'

'We had sex,' Matt told her. 'You could be carrying my child.'

Matt's child.

Harriet felt her heart beat a sharply painful tattoo of longing.

'No!' she whispered, shaking her head. Her mouth

had suddenly gone dry and she had to wet her lips with the tip of her tongue. 'That's not possible…you used a condom.'

Matt gave her a derisory look. 'That's no guarantee!'

What on earth had he started? The fierce mule kick his words had brought to his emotions had activated a response in his body that told him how much it was now wanting to ensure that his unfounded threat became an absolute certainty. A child; Harriet's body swelling with his child.

Harriet felt as though she was drowning in her own sickening panic.

'No. *No.* You can't make me. I *won't* marry you, Matt. Not even if I am pregnant. I…I couldn't bear it.'

Matt went perfectly still as he heard the emotional agony in her voice. His own emotion carved twin deep grooves of biting loss along either side of his mouth, but Harriet was too caught up in her feelings to notice. He marched towards the private lift that serviced his apartment, aware that Harriet was following him.

Savagely he pressed the button and the doors opened immediately.

'Don't do this to me, Matt,' she begged as she got in the lift with him and the doors shut behind them. 'I couldn't bear being married to you when I love you so much and you don't love me at all. In fact I think it would kill me.'

There was a sharp, tense silence, and then Matt asked very quietly, 'Would you like to repeat what you just said?'

Harriet closed her eyes and gulped in air.

'You heard me.'

'You love me so much…?' Matt prompted her.

'Yes,' she whispered in defeat.

'And I don't love you at all?'

Matt reached behind him for the 'stop' button and pressed it hard.

Harriet gasped in shock as the lift's abrupt halt threw her against him. No, not against him, she recognised dizzily, but into him—into his open arms, which wrapped tightly around her, whilst his mouth fastened hungrily on hers in a fierce claim of possession.

'Wrong!' Matt corrected her thickly against her mouth when he was finally able to release it. 'I do love you. I have loved you and I shall love you more deeply, more passionately, than I ever thought it was possible for me to love anyone.'

'You love me?' The miracle of hope began to edge into her voice.

Matt groaned and took her back in his arms, releasing the lift button as he did so.

He was still kissing her when the doors opened.

'Have we reached the penthouse?' Harriet asked dizzily.

Matt turned his head and glanced into the office behind them—to see his staff working very hard at not noticing their intimacy.

'Not exactly,' he answered.

Uncertainly Harriet turned her head.

'Matt, everyone can see us!' she whispered, pink-cheeked.

'Yes, they can,' he agreed, still holding her in his arms. Obviously he'd pressed 'stop' before the lift had started moving, and now the doors had opened automatically. 'And what they can see is that you are mine.'

'I never loved Ben the way you thought,' Harriet told him truthfully. 'I've never loved anyone the way I love you, Matt. It wasn't true what I said about…about going to bed with you to prove to you I wasn't saving myself for Ben either,' she added huskily. 'I wanted you like that the moment I saw you.' Her body shuddered in visible longing. 'In fact I think I fell in love with you the moment I saw you, but you were so…so cold towards me…'

'Was I? It must have been something to do with all those cold showers I kept on having to take,' he teased her, changing tack to ask, 'How do you feel about a June wedding?'

'June?' Dismay darkened her eyes. 'But it's already May, and that means waiting a whole year.

'I mean *this* June,' Matt corrected her softly, firmly closing the lift door.

'Where are we going now?' Harriet asked.

'To heaven,' he answered thickly, 'via the penthouse. Unless you really want to know what it's like to make love in a lift?'

'Oh, Matt it's the same suite!'

Harriet's eyes shone with love and a longing that made Matt's hands tremble slightly as he locked the suite door and turned to walk towards her.

'I wanted us to celebrate our true engagement here, where we both made our commitment to one another, even though then we didn't know we shared those feelings. Harriet, come here. I can't bear not having you in my arms a second longer.'

'What about the champagne?' Harriet protested.

'And the canapés and the chocolate coated strawberries…?'

'What's that look for?' she demanded, when Matt suddenly started to smile as he remembered what he had wanted to do that first night she had so innocently tormented him.

When he told her she blushed and laughed, and then whispered to him that she'd like to reciprocate but that she loved the taste of him so much she didn't want to dilute it with champagne.

'Harriet…' he groaned unevenly.

'I don't know how I'm going to bear sleeping without you for three whole days when we go home for the wedding,' Harriet said, tugging at his shirt buttons and nuzzling her lips against his skin.

'We'll be able to make up for it once we're on honeymoon,' Matt promised.

'Mmm…a whole month of just the two of us.' Harriet shuddered with eager pleasure, and then sighed happily as she succeeded in unfastening his shirt.

EPILOGUE

'OH, LOOK at the bride—isn't she beautiful?' the little girl called out in excitement as she stood on the pavement watching the bridal party arrive.

Harriet could see her father's proud smile as she walked towards the church on his arm.

It was a perfect June day, and the ivory silk gown she and her mother had chosen together moved softly in the warm summer air.

Her brother and his wife and children had flown over from America for the occasion, and behind her she could hear Ben speaking sternly to her small niece and nephew, reminding them of their important duties as flower girl and page boy.

A smile curled Harriet's mouth.

She knew it was unusual for her to have a male supporter as part of the bridal party, but Ben was her best friend and Matt had totally agreed with her wish to honour that friendship by asking Ben to be her supporter and Cindi to be her bridesmaid.

'Of course you will have to wear pink,' Harriet had told Ben gravely.

'Over my dead body.' Ben had refused point-blank—until he had realised she had been teasing him.

The church doors opened and Harriet stepped from the sunlight into the porch. The organ music swelled and Harriet walked as slowly as she could down the aisle on her father's arm—when in reality she wanted to run to Matt as fast as she could.

Around her the pews were filled with family and friends, but Harriet was oblivious to everyone but Matt. Matt was now her family, her friend, her all and her everything.

Unconventionally he was standing facing her, watching her draw closer to him, and when she reached him they looked at one another, sharing an intimate moment of silent commitment and promise.

The familiar words of the marriage service began. 'Dearly beloved…'

Matt was hers; for now and forever.

Carole Mortimer

HIS DARLING VALENTINE

CHAPTER ONE

WHAT the—!

In the process of stepping out of her own front doorway, Tazzy came to an abrupt halt, instead staring down wide-eyed at the tiny kitten that sat in a basket on the doorstep.

Where on earth had it come from? More to the point, what was it doing here?

Well, one thing was for certain, it hadn't arrived here of its own volition; a stray kitten did not come complete with basket, bowl, and sachets of food. Or with a red ribbon tied in a neat bow about its tiny neck!

Tazzy bent down to look at the ball of grey fluff, suddenly finding herself the focus of startled blue eyes as it became aware of her presence.

'Hey, it's okay,' she soothed as the tiny thing leapt to its feet in surprise, holding out her hand—for it to either lick or scratch, depending on whether it saw her as friend or foe.

While it made up its mind, Tazzy took the opportunity to glance up and down the street. As expected, at seven-thirty in the morning, it was totally deserted. The lights were on in several of the houses, but all the cars were still in the driveways. Only Tazzy, it seemed, with her innate sense of responsibility, left the house at seven-thirty in the morning in order to be at her desk by eight-fifteen. There was certainly no one visible who could possibly have delivered the kitten to her doorstep.

She gave a start of surprise herself as she felt the moist rasp of a minute tongue on the back of her hand, the kitten jumping back too at this sudden movement.

'We could go on like this all morning.' She laughed, reaching out to pick the kitten up, absolutely enchanted by the way the little ball of fur, its face looking at her so trustingly, fitted neatly into the palm of her hand.

But even as Tazzy acknowledged that she noticed the small white card attached to the red ribbon. 'To Anastasia. With love', the card read.

How very peculiar. No one ever called her by her full name of Anastasia, in fact most people weren't even aware that was her actual name. And why on earth would someone give her a kitten, with or without love? Christmas had been and gone, and her birthday wasn't until August.

Not that it mattered why someone had thought she would appreciate having a pet, she simply couldn't keep the kitten. She was Personal Assistant to Ross Valentine, a computer software troubleshooter of unparalleled skill. His business took him all over the world, and Tazzy usually accompanied Ross on those trips, which didn't allow for attachments of any kind.

Talking of which, what was she going to do with the kitten today while she was at work?

The frown deepened between clear green eyes. She might not be able to keep it, but she couldn't just leave the poor little thing out here in the cold, either; it might wander off and get itself lost, or worse—run over. And she certainly couldn't take it with her—she could already imagine the look of surprise on Ross's face if she were to arrive at his house, their place of work as well as Ross's home, with the kitten in tow!

She really didn't have any choice; she would just have to make it comfortable in the kitchen until she returned later, when she could turn her mind to finding somewhere—or someone—who would take the kitten off her hands.

'I'm sorry, but that's just the way it is,' she told the kitten ruefully as it continued to look up at her with those trusting blue eyes.

It took her a few minutes to take off the bow, to make the kitchen safe and put out food for the tiny creature, by which time, she realized agitatedly, she was going to be late into work this morning.

The traffic, usually minimal at that early hour, was already starting to build up by the time she finally got on the road, Tazzy's tension building along with it.

Consequently, she was not her usual calm, collected self when she finally made it into her office at eight-thirty. Her agitation deepened as she found Ross Valentine already standing beside her desk, a pile of her carefully logged files in his hand, files Tazzy knew from experience would no longer be in any sort of order. Served her right for being late, she inwardly remonstrated with herself.

Being a computer expert, Ross had pooh-poohed the fact that she kept everything on paper as well as on disk, but as her system had saved him work on several occasions when his computer had crashed, he had stopped mentioning how antiquated her own system was.

Ross raised dark brows now over eyes the colour

of sherry. 'Dare I say that you're looking less than your usual unflustered self this morning, Miss Darling?' he mocked, those brows shooting up even further as Tazzy, her cheeks flushed, scowled at him in reply. 'Perhaps not,' he muttered under his breath.

Tazzy wordlessly took down the hanger from behind the door, carefully hanging her outer coat on it before replacing it neatly back on the hook. She smoothed back the neat chignon of her copper-coloured hair before moving to switch on the coffee percolator that stood on top of one of the filing cabinets, using the normality of her usual morning routine to try to bring some calm to her day, totally thrown by the fact that Ross had appeared in her office before her.

The day had not started well, with the mysterious arrival of that kitten on her doorstep—and being late for work certainly didn't improve matters!

Ross Valentine watched her as she moved efficiently about the room, preparing a coffee tray for him and a separate cup for herself. 'Tell me, Miss Darling, how long have you worked for me now?' he asked, arms folded across the muscled width of his chest.

Tazzy turned to give him a puzzled frown. 'I don't understand—'

'Just answer the question, hmm?' he encouraged lightly.

'I believe it's eighteen months, Mr Valentine,' she said smartly.

Eighteen months, one week, and half an hour, to be exact. And she had been in love with this man, it seemed, for every minute of that time!

She loved the way his dark hair was inclined to

curl slightly if he forgot to get it cut—which was often!—the deep sherry-brown of his eyes, eyes that became incredibly warm when he smiled. His high cheekbones gave him a slightly foreign appearance, his nose was long and aristocratic, and his sensual mouth was wide above the squareness of his jaw. His body was athletically slim, and as for his hands—! More than once she had sat and daydreamed about what it would feel like to have those long, slender hands move caressingly over her body...

She loved his sense of humour too, the closeness he had maintained with his parents, despite having lived in this house on his own, apart from the house-keeper, the last ten years. Sylvia and Nigel Valentine were frequent visitors to the house Ross used to work in as well as live in, two rooms that overlooked the back garden having been converted into offices for both Ross and Tazzy.

Having been orphaned at five years old herself, and brought up by an elderly maiden aunt who had died five years ago when Tazzy was twenty, she rather envied Ross his warm family life.

But none of her thoughts or love for this man showed in her expression now as she continued to look at him enquiringly.

Ross nodded. 'And in all of that time how many times have you failed to be seated at your desk by eight-fifteen in the morning?'

She eyed him warily. 'Just this morning,' she finally replied, still uncertain as to what point he was trying to make; either he was about to sack her for being late, or congratulate her for never having been so before!

'Exactly,' he acknowledged dryly. 'So why are you

skulking around the room as if you expect me to fire you at any moment?'

Because by arriving at eight-fifteen every morning she gave herself enough time to tidy her appearance, check e-mails, and be her normal efficient self by the time Ross usually came in at eight forty-five. The arrival of that kitten on her doorstep had completely thrown her normal routine into disarray—and Tazzy along with it! She simply wasn't her usual calm, controlled self this morning, which made her feel slightly defensive.

'I—something happened to delay me this morning. Someone left me—left a present on the doorstep for me,' she explained.

'It's the day for it, isn't it?' Ross shrugged.

Tazzy frowned. 'Day for what—? Oh.' She broke off abruptly as she suddenly realized exactly what day it was.

The fourteenth of February. Valentine's Day. And the kitten had had a red bow tied about its tiny neck, the gift card that accompanied it unsigned…

Ross nodded. 'So what did you get?' he prompted interestedly, making himself comfortable on the side of her desk. 'Red roses? A cuddly teddy bear? A box of chocolates? Or perhaps some sexy underwear—'

'It was a kitten,' she cut in sharply, embarrassed colour in her cheeks at his last suggestion.

The only way she had been able to cope with loving Ross in the way that she did was to maintain a certain formality in their relationship, insisting on calling him Mr Valentine, and having him always refer to her as Miss Darling. Having him talk about 'sexy underwear' was not conducive to that formality!

'A kitten?' Ross repeated incredulously. 'I had no idea you liked cats.'

'I'm not sure that I do,' she answered slowly, at the same time aware that the defenceless ball of fur left on her doorstep earlier had already made a dent in her heart. 'I told you, it was a present,' she added.

A Valentine present...

But who from? Oh, she had dated often before coming to work for Ross Valentine eighteen months ago, occasionally accepted invitations even now, if only to stop other people from drawing their own conclusions concerning her single status when her boss was so obviously an extremely eligible bachelor of thirty-seven. But the fact that she rarely dated the same person twice meant that she now had no idea who could have placed the kitten outside her front door!

'What are you going to do with it?' Ross looked amused.

Good question. The truth was, she had no idea, very much aware that her job as Ross Valentine's Personal Assistant, travelling around the world with him, did not even allow for the luxury of owning a goldfish.

But, at the same time, she couldn't shake off the vision of that endearing little face, the tiny black nose, those beautiful blue eyes that had gazed up at her so appealingly earlier as she'd left the kitten in the warm snugness of her kitchen.

But, tempted as she might be, there was no way she could keep it!

'I have no idea,' she answered honestly. 'Try to find someone who will take it in, I suppose.'

'I'll take it if you don't want it,' Ross offered.

Tazzy stared at him in surprise. Admittedly, he had the luxury of a housekeeper who could look after the kitten any time he had to be away on business. But even so…

'I haven't definitely decided what I'm going to do with him yet,' she resisted.

'Or her,' Ross pointed out.

Tazzy frowned. 'Or her,' she acknowledged slowly, having no idea whether it was a she or a he! 'But its name is Shadow,' she added without thinking.

Now exactly where had that come from? She hadn't even been aware until the word had come out of her mouth that she had actually named the kitten!

When she had finally left the house this morning, the kitten safely ensconced in the kitchen, she had had every intention of delivering it to a cat sanctuary when she returned home later on this evening. Ross's offer to take the kitten off her hands seemed to have brought out a possessive streak in her.

Ross smiled, brown eyes warm. 'You named it already.'

Tazzy once again felt flustered. 'Not really. I—Shadow would do for a boy or a girl, though.'

'So it would,' he agreed, standing up.

Allowing Tazzy to breathe normally once again. Outwardly, she managed to remain efficient and professional in front of this man, but inwardly, whenever Ross was close, she felt a constriction in her throat, a fluttering in her chest. It didn't exactly make for calm working conditions—but the thought of not working for Ross was completely unacceptable to her.

'I'll bring your coffee through in a moment,' she told him with cool dismissal.

'Thanks.' He nodded. 'Could you bring the e-mails through when you're ready, too?'

'Of course, Mr Valentine,' she answered briskly, finding her usual confidence in adopting her role as his PA.

'Oh, and Tazzy...?' He paused before moving away.

She looked up at him with calm enquiry, deciding to ignore his slip of addressing her by her Christian name in preference to hastening his departure.

'Happy Valentine's Day,' he murmured huskily, bending his head and briefly brushing his lips against hers. 'Mmm, nice,' he said appreciatively, hands lightly cupping each side of her face. 'In fact, it was so nice, I think I'll do it again,' he added softly before his lips claimed hers a second time, a lingering kiss this time as he tasted and sipped the softness of her lips.

Tazzy was too stunned to do any more than kiss him back, her lips tingling from the touch of Ross's, her body trembling with rising desire, breasts uptilted as they pressed against the hardness of his chest.

Finally, when Tazzy felt as if her knees were about to give way completely, Ross raised his head to look down at her. 'Happy Valentine's Day, Tazzy,' he murmured again before moving away to leave the room, softly closing the connecting door behind him.

Leaving Tazzy in a state of total shock!

CHAPTER TWO

WELL—!

For the second time that morning Tazzy found herself at a complete loss for words. And it wasn't even nine o'clock yet!

She moved to sit down abruptly in her chair behind the desk, moving a hand up to tentatively touch lips that still tingled from contact with Ross's.

Not by word or deed had he ever before stepped over that line between employer/employee. Leaving Tazzy to wonder why he should have done so now… She didn't—

'Tazzy, could I have the file on the Hanson hotel chain?' Ross stood in the open doorway between their two offices, his manner completely businesslike now.

Just as if those kisses, that melting touch of his lips on Tazzy's, had never happened!

He raised dark brows at her silence. 'Today, if possible?' he teased.

She stood up abruptly, inwardly urging herself to pull herself together; Ross Valentine was far from the first man to kiss her, for goodness' sake. But at the same time, he was the first man she had ever been in love with who had kissed her!

'Yes, of course, Mr Valentine.' She moved to one of the filing cabinets that stood along one wall of her office.

At least, that was what she intended doing—until she sensed that Ross still stood in the doorway, leaning nonchalantly against the frame as he made no effort to hide the fact he was watching her every move.

Making Tazzy feel extremely self-conscious! 'I'll bring it through once I've found it,' she assured him sharply.

'Fine,' he accepted, making no effort to move. 'You know, Tazzy—'

'I thought we had agreed that it was much more suitable, during our hours of working together, if we stick to Mr Valentine and Miss Darling?' she reminded him coolly. Goodness knew it was strange enough actually working in this man's house, without being any more familiar with each other.

She had thought it an unconventional arrangement when she'd first come for her job interview eighteen months ago, but once she had met Ross Valentine she would have agreed to work out in the garden shed!

'As I remember it, you were the one to come up with that particular rule,' Ross drawled. 'Personally, I've always thought it sounded very unfriendly.'

'Unfamiliar,' Tazzy corrected briskly, at the same time whipping the appropriate file from the drawer and holding it out to him. 'I really do think that it's best during office hours.'

He took the file, his expression one of reproach. 'Well, as we don't seem to have any "out of office hours," when do I get to call you Tazzy?'

Her eyes widened with impatience. 'You don't.' That was the whole idea, for goodness' sake!

She wasn't sure, spending as much time as she did in his company, often travelling abroad together for several days at a time, if she would be able to cope with working for him at all if she hadn't put up some sort of barrier of formality between them from the first.

'I'm not sure I particularly care for that,' he pondered.

She looked at him in exasperation. 'Mr Valentine—'

'Tazzy Darling?' he came back blandly, dark brows raised in innocent query.

Her exasperation deepened. Not that she wasn't used to her surname being the butt of jokes, had been teased about it unmercifully ever since she'd first started school; it was just that she wasn't used to her employer resorting to such inanity.

'Miss Darling will do,' she said impatiently. 'I—' She broke off as a knock sounded on her office door, Ross's housekeeper opening the door seconds later to admit the man who accompanied her.

At least, Tazzy presumed it was a man. It was a little hard to tell when he—she?—was carrying the hugest bouquet of red roses Tazzy had ever seen in her life!

'The gentleman has instructions to deliver the roses personally,' Mrs Brown, the housekeeper, explained apologetically.

Tazzy turned accusing eyes on Ross Valentine; she knew that he dated occasionally, but none of those women seemed to last very long—which begged the question, which one of them had sent him this huge bouquet of red roses for Valentine's Day? Honestly, it was totally out of—

'Miss Darling?' the delivery man prompted as he looked at her hopefully.

Tazzy turned slowly to look at the man, her tone wary as she answered him. 'Yes...?'

The man nodded his satisfaction with her answer. 'Then these are for you.' He placed the bouquet into her unresisting arms. 'Whoever he is, he must have it real bad!' he added, giving a knowing wink in Tazzy's direction before departing the room, Mrs Brown following behind him.

Tazzy didn't move. Couldn't move. Could only stare at what had to be dozens of deep red roses in her arms.

There had to have been some sort of mistake. These flowers couldn't possibly be for her. She never received roses, on Valentine's Day, or any other day.

But thinking of Valentine...

She glanced across at her employer, a blush warming her cheeks as she saw he was looking straight back at her, dark brows raised in a question.

That look was enough to shake Tazzy out of the daze she had lapsed into on being presented with the red roses. 'I think there must have been some mistake, and these were meant for you.' She grimaced as she held out the flowers to him.

Ross shook his head, making no effort to take the blood-red blooms from her. 'He distinctly said they were for Miss Darling, and as we both know that's you...' He strolled over to pluck out the white card that nestled amongst the roses. '"To Anastasia. Much love,"' he read out. 'No, they're definitely for you, Tazzy.' He grinned teasingly. 'As the man said, someone's got it bad,' he added with an appreciative glance at the dozens of roses.

To Anastasia. Much love...

The card attached to the kitten earlier this morning

had read, 'To Anastasia. With love.' The messages were so similar that it was impossible not to wonder if the kitten and the roses hadn't been sent to her by the same person. But if so, who could that person be?

She had no idea!

She really didn't. Oh, several of the men she had met while travelling with Ross had flirted with her or paid her compliments, but she was certain that none of them knew her name was Anastasia.

The postman occasionally paid her a compliment when she went to the door to collect the mail from him, as did the young man from the courier service they habitually used, but as there had to be at least fifty red roses here, delivered on Valentine's Day too, Tazzy would hazard a guess at such an extravagant gesture of love being out of either of their financial leagues. No, she really had no idea who could have sent them to her.

Neither did she appreciate their being delivered here at her place of work, in front of Ross, of all people; on today's evidence he was going to believe there was someone serious in her life!

'Have you been holding out on me, Miss Darling?' Ross's next words seemed to confirm that particular worry. 'You aren't thinking of leaving me in order to get married, by any chance?' he asked.

'Certainly not!' Tazzy dropped the roses down onto her desktop as if she had been pricked by one of their thorns. 'I think someone must be playing a practical joke on me,' she excused lamely.

'An expensive practical joke,' Ross disagreed with a shake of his head. 'No, Tazzy—Miss Darling,' he corrected himself as she gave him a pointed look, 'I think you should look at the distinct possibility that you have a secret admirer.' He lightly touched one of the velvety soft flowers.

Then whoever it was had kept it such a secret that she didn't have a clue as to who it could possibly be!

'Don't be ridiculous,' she snapped, deciding that office protocol had been broken enough for one day. 'I have some work to do,' she added pointedly when Ross still made no effort to leave but continued to look at her speculatively.

'I think, Miss Darling,' he finally murmured consideringly, 'that you and I ought to have lunch together today in order to discuss the possibility of someone stealing you away from me, don't you?'

She glared at him. 'I told you, there is nothing to discuss!'

Ross shook his head. 'I disagree.'

Oh, great, not only did she not know who was indulging in these ridiculous Valentine pranks, but now she had to try and explain it to her employer!

She gave a heavy sigh. 'I'll ask Mrs Brown to make us both some sandwiches.' It would be far from the first time Tazzy had worked through her lunch-hour.

'No, I don't think so.'

Tazzy gave a puzzled frown. 'You would prefer me to ask her to prepare something else?' A cooked lunch would save her the problem of cooking for herself this evening when she got home. In view of the fact that she had to do something about the kitten, that arrangement could work out quite well.

Ross smiled as he shook his head. 'I would *prefer* it if we went out somewhere to eat. What's the name of that little place you occasionally go to with that friend of yours—Anne, isn't it?—that sometimes calls for you here?'

'Luigi's?' Tazzy supplied with a frown.

'That's the place!' His smile deepened. 'We'll go there for lunch.'

For one thing, Luigi's was a small Italian bistro, hardly the sort of place Ross usually frequented, with his accumulated wealth and preference for French cuisine. For another, she did not relish the idea of going there with Ross only to bump into her friend Anne— who did go to Luigi's often. Knowing Anne, she would demand to know all the details the next time the two of them met! What was wrong with Mrs Brown's cooking anyway? It had always been good enough before!

Then she remembered...

'Have you forgotten what day it is today?' she reminded Ross.

'That would be a little difficult, wouldn't it, when your office is full of red roses?' He gave the long-stemmed blooms a pointed look.

Tazzy felt the warmth in her cheeks. 'Hardly full,' she said, shifting the bouquet to one side of her desk. 'I was actually trying to point out to you that there is no way we will get a table at Luigi's for lunch today. He was fully booked weeks ago.'

'He was?' Ross looked startled by this information.

Tazzy found it quite endearing that it obviously hadn't even occurred to him that almost all restaurants would be fully booked today, both at lunch-time and this evening; apparently he had never tried to take anyone out to lunch on Valentine's Day before!

'Okay, forget Luigi's,' Ross dismissed impatiently.

Tazzy nodded. 'Shall I ask Mrs Brown to get us both a sandwich, after all?'

'Certainly not!' he said firmly. 'I invited you out to lunch, and out we will most definitely go.'

'But—'

'Leave it to me,' Ross interrupted. 'I'll book us a table somewhere for lunch.'

Her eyes widened. 'You will?'

'I will.' He nodded, his expression becoming mocking at her obvious surprise. 'Tazzy, believe it or not, before the advent of your undoubtedly efficient self into my life, I was quite capable of telephoning a restaurant myself and booking my own table!'

She knew that he still did that if he was taking a woman out to dinner. Something, in view of her own feelings towards him, she had always been grateful for.

But that wasn't the point she had been about to make; it was the fact that this didn't sound like a business lunch to her, and the two of them having lunch together under any other circumstances was not a good idea...

'I'm sure you were,' she soothed. 'It's just that—'

'I said leave it to me, Tazzy,' Ross insisted, moving towards the connecting door.

'Use the intercom the next time you need something,' Tazzy was stung into advising him sharply as he was closing the door, inwardly wondering when the strangeness of today was going to end!

The door opened again, Ross grimacing across at her. 'I loathe that damned intercom,' he muttered. 'I rue the day I ever let you persuade me into having it installed.'

She was well aware of Ross's feelings concerning the intercom system between their two offices. But, for her part, it was yet another move to keep their relationship on a businesslike footing; before the intercom had been installed Ross had been altogether too fond of just wandering into her office whenever he felt like it, sitting on the side of her desk to discuss whatever problem was bothering him at the time. And in the process usually managing to upset Tazzy's equilibrium for at least half an hour after he had left— by which time he had usually wandered back in again! The intercom system had stopped all of that. At least…until today, it had…

'Nevertheless, it's there to be used,' she insisted primly.

'So was the guillotine!' Ross pointed out. 'And we all know what use that was put to! Not all machines are progress, you know, Tazzy.'

This sounded more than slightly ridiculous coming from a man who specialized in clearing any glitch or bug that might attack a computer or its software!

He had also called her by her first name yet again! It was way past time this familiarity was put to an end!

'I'm afraid I really can't have lunch with you today,' she told him determinedly. 'I have to go and check on the kitten,' she explained as he gave her a frowning look.

His brow cleared. 'We'll both go,' he offered. 'We can go on to the restaurant from there.'

Tazzy stared at him. Never once during the eighteen months she'd worked for him had there been a need for him to go to her home. 'I don't think—'

'Oh, come on, Tazzy,' he encouraged. 'After all, I might end up taking the kitten off your hands.'

'I told you, I haven't decided yet whether or not

I'm going to keep it myself!' she came back defensively.

'Going to wait and see who gave him to you first, is that it?' Ross teased, brown eyes definitely laughing at her.

'Certainly not,' she denied crossly. 'Oh, very well, you can come with me at lunch-time,' she capitulated. 'You'll just have to excuse the mess,' she added ungraciously, knowing there was no mess, that she kept her home as tidy as she kept her office.

But the thought of Ross in her home, the one place she never had to remember him having been, was not a pleasant one. Her little terraced house was her sanctuary. A sanctuary that was about to be invaded!

'I'll do that.' Ross grinned knowingly. 'While we're there, you could also change into something a little less…businesslike,' he added before continuing on his way to his own office.

Tazzy glared at the now closed door between the two rooms. She had no intention of changing into something less businesslike! Businesslike was how she liked to be whenever she was around Ross, and she had no intention of ever changing that.

Whoever the practical joker was who had sent her first the kitten, and then these roses, had a lot to answer for. Because she had no doubts that it was the anonymous gifts she had received today that had prompted Ross into inviting her out to lunch, if only to try and find out from Tazzy exactly how serious the relationship was.

When there was no relationship!

CHAPTER THREE

'PIERRE will be more than pleased to see us both at about one-thirty,' Ross told Tazzy with satisfaction as he strolled back into her office a couple of hours later.

Pierre Gaston owned one of the most select restaurants in London, with extortionate prices to go along with that prestige; no doubt he would be pleased to see another two customers in his restaurant at lunchtime!

But, Tazzy noted with a certain inner smugness, it had taken Ross almost two hours to come up with a restaurant that had availability.

Although the fact that it was Pierre's meant she might just have to rethink her decision not to change out of the grey suit and white blouse she had worn for work today. The women that frequented such a restaurant had a totally different idea of 'power dressing' from the one she had: designer suits and diamonds, probably!

'You were right about everywhere being full,' Ross admitted with a grimace as he came over to sit on the side of her desk. 'I tried Pierre's as a last resort.'

That was one of the endearing qualities about Ross that so made her love him; he hadn't needed to admit to her that he had found difficulty, after all, but he had done so anyway.

'Not that you aren't worth it,' he hastened to add

with a boyish smile. 'I just had somewhere a little more—well, less formal, let's say—in mind.'

'There really is no need to take me out at all,' she assured him, calmer now than she had been a couple of hours ago. Everything was back under control, even the red roses were out of the way on top of a filing cabinet in a couple of vases she had borrowed from Mrs Brown; she simply hadn't the heart to throw such beautiful flowers in the bin—whoever they might have come from! 'I can promise you, I'm not involved in a relationship, and have no intention of letting anyone ''steal me away'' from your employment,' she added impatiently.

He shrugged. 'The roses say differently.'

Admittedly, the roses, five dozen of them in all— Tazzy had counted them as she'd put them in the vases!—must have cost someone a small fortune, especially today of all days, but, as she couldn't even take a wild guess at who might have sent them, the gesture was totally wasted on her!

She shook her head. 'Couldn't you just take my word for it that they don't? It would save you having to go to the expense of taking me out to lunch.'

'No, I said I was taking you out, and that's what I'm going to do,' Ross insisted. 'So we had better leave here—' He broke off as the second knock of the morning sounded on Tazzy's office door, a rather bemused Mrs Brown once again the perpetrator, another man trailing in her wake.

Tazzy had tensed the moment the knock had sounded on the door, and as she saw the enormous box of chocolates the man carried in his hands—a red heart-shaped box of chocolates, tied up with a red ribbon—she knew she was right to feel that way!

She closed her eyes, hoping—and praying!—that the chocolates hadn't come from her mystery admirer too, that they weren't even for her. Although perhaps, in the circumstances, that would be hoping for too much!

Mrs Brown looked even more bemused than she had earlier. 'This gentleman has instructions to deliver the chocolates personally, too,' she told them.

'Miss Darling?' The man looked at Tazzy enquiringly.

'Yes,' she confirmed abruptly, unable to even look at Ross this time as the delivery man crossed the room to place the box of chocolates into her hands—goodness knew what Ross was making of all this! 'Thank you,' she said stiffly.

The man grinned. 'Eleven o'clock the man said, and eleven o'clock it is,' he said with satisfaction.

Tazzy's gaze narrowed. 'What man?'

'Oh, the office didn't tell me that, love,' the man replied jovially, shaking his head. 'I'm just the delivery man, you see.'

No help there, then, with the identity of this mystery admirer. Pity. For a moment there—

'Here.' Ross moved forward to tip the man.

'Oh, no, guv'nor, that was already taken care of when the chocolates were given to us for delivery,' the man explained.

Tazzy was so stunned by this second Valentine delivery to her place of work that she hadn't even thought about tipping the man. The fact that he refused Ross's attempt to do so, because he had already received a tip, was doubly odd. The mystery admirer was taking no chances on having his identity discovered, was he?

Which was strange in itself. Surely the whole point of gifts on Valentine's Day was that the person receiving them should eventually realize who they had come from? After all, there wasn't a lot of point to the exercise otherwise.

But it wasn't even lunch-time yet, Tazzy reminded herself; plenty of time left yet today for the man to somehow show himself as the giver of these gifts.

'Thank you,' she told the delivery man once again before he left with Mrs Brown, still unable to actually look at Ross as he stood silently across the room, wishing that he hadn't been in the room when this second delivery had been made.

At least then she might have stood some chance of hiding these chocolates from him—although quite where she would be able to hide such a huge box, she had no idea!

This was all so ridiculous. *She* felt ridiculous. And she couldn't even begin to guess at Ross's feelings!

'Aren't you going to open them?' he encouraged hopefully. 'They're my favourites. And we aren't going to be having lunch for at least another couple of hours.'

Tazzy didn't answer him immediately, staring down at the white card that had been tucked beneath the red ribbon. 'To Anastasia. With affection and love.' Affection as well as love now!

Strangely, she found the claim of affection more confusing than the love; surely to feel affection for someone they had to know that person rather well? Which begged the question, how could some man feel this way about her and she not even know about it?

Well, she knew about it now—and she wished that she didn't.

'You open them.' She thrust the box across the desk towards Ross. 'I'm starting to think that whoever this man is he must be some sort of a crackpot!'

A kitten, red roses, and now a heart-shaped box of chocolates; where was it all going to end?

Ross chuckled as he began to undo the ribbon that secured the box. 'I'm sure most women don't think that when they receive gifts from a man.'

She wasn't 'most women,' and it was the fact that she had no idea who the man was that made her feel so confused. Besides, if this continued, Ross was never going to believe her when she kept insisting there was no one serious in her life!

She might stand absolutely no chance of ever having her love for him returned, but at least she could work with him, see him almost every day, and that was better than nothing.

'You keep the chocolates, as they're your favourite brand,' she told him stiltedly.

'Oh, I couldn't do that, Tazzy,' he refused. 'After all, how would you explain not having them?'

She frowned. 'To whom?'

'Your admirer, of course,' Ross reproved teasingly.

'I don't have an admirer!' she bit out through gritted teeth.

'Of course you do,' Ross contradicted, sitting on the edge of the desk to lift the lid of the box of chocolates. 'Ah.' He paused. 'Tazzy...?'

'What is it now?' she sighed, so weary from all of this that she just wanted to put her head on her arms on the desktop and go to sleep—or weep! 'Don't tell me, there aren't any chocolates in the box, just empty papers!' In truth, she really would prefer that this was a practical joke rather than someone seriously secretly in love with her.

Because she was never going to be in love with any man but Ross...

'Oh, no, there's chocolates,' he assured her. 'But there's also this.'

'This,' Tazzy found out seconds later as Ross lifted it up for her to see, turned out to be a gold chain with a gold heart suspended on it!

'Certainly not one of the usual fillings to these particular chocolates,' he murmured with amusement. 'Let's put it on and see how it looks—'

'No!' Tazzy protested sharply as Ross would have stood up to fasten the chain about the slenderness of her neck. 'Let's not.' She stared at the necklace as if it were a snake about to strike her.

Ross frowned. 'But you never wear jewellery. And this is rather a beautiful necklace, even if I do say so myself.' Once again he made a move to stand up.

'I said no, Ross.' Tazzy raised a protesting hand.

She never wore jewellery because she couldn't afford jewellery. It was all she could do to feed herself, pay her mortgage, and maintain and run her car, let alone spend her money on frivolous things like jewellery!

She stood up abruptly. 'I don't want it,' she told him flatly. 'If I want a necklace, I'll buy it myself,' she added at his puzzled look, 'not accept it from a complete stranger.'

Ross relaxed back on the desk, the gold chain still dangling from his fingers as he looked up at her. 'Obviously this man doesn't want the two of you to remain strangers,' he said slowly.

Her eyes flashed deeply green as she glared at him.

'Then he can behave like any other man would have done, in the circumstances, and introduce himself—not use the excuse of Valentine's Day to send me an assortment of expensive and impractical gifts!

Ross looked at her quizzically for several long seconds, finally giving a shake of his head. 'You know, Tazzy, I don't think I'll ever understand women. The man has done everything to show you how he feels but propose—and you still don't want to know!'

'Of course I want to know,' she snapped. 'I want to know who on earth he is—if only so I can give back his expensive presents.'

Ross shrugged. 'Maybe he doesn't want them back.'

'Don't you understand? I don't care what he wants!' Her voice rose in her agitation.

'No, Tazzy, I really *don't* understand…' he said.

'Then that makes two of us!' She breathed out heavily.

He shook his head. 'Most women that I know would be at least flattered by this—attention. And if not flattered, then amused. You just seem angry.'

Maybe that was because she *was* angry! Because this was sending out all the wrong messages to Ross. The man she was in love with.

'After all,' Ross continued, 'you seem to like the kitten well enough. And the roses are beautiful. Is it that you don't like this particular brand of chocolates?'

Tazzy looked at him in astonishment. Could he really not see—? No, she acknowledged wryly, of course he couldn't see why it was that she was so angry. Because, despite those kisses earlier this morning, he didn't see her as anything other than his efficient PA!

And she would do well to remember that... 'I like them fine,' she answered in a calmer voice. 'And perhaps you're right,' she added ruefully. 'Perhaps I should find all of this amusing.'

'Hmm.' He nodded consideringly. 'But perhaps not too amusing. After all, the man must have his feelings too,' he reasoned.

He might have, but those feelings were causing her severe embarrassment!

'Never mind, let's just forget about it for now.' She glanced at her watch. 'Do you think we should leave now? After all, I have to check on the kitten before we go to lunch.'

Ross nodded, standing up. 'What do you intend doing with this?' He held the necklace up pointedly.

Tazzy took it from him, carefully placing it back inside the box before replacing the lid. 'When—if,' she corrected heavily, 'I ever get to meet the man who sent me these, I shall make sure it is safely returned to him.'

He raised an eyebrow. 'If that's the way you feel about it.'

'It is,' she said with finality, moving to collect her coat from the back of the door. 'Are we going in your car or mine?' She stood ready to leave.

'Mine. But give me five minutes, will you?' He turned to go back to his own office. 'Perhaps you could use the time to go and explain things to Mrs Brown?' he suggested teasingly. 'The poor woman was looking completely befuddled earlier!' he added before going through to his office.

Mrs Brown was befuddled? How did he think Tazzy felt?

She gave one last lingering glance at the box of chocolates, easily able to envisage the beautiful necklace that nestled inside it. No one had ever given her jewellery before. And it was such a beautiful necklace, with an old-fashioned style that appealed to her, the heart a solid piece of gold.

Oh, well…

It would have to go back, and that was the end of the matter.

Pity…

CHAPTER FOUR

'THIS is nice,' Ross commented admiringly as he looked around the comfort of Tazzy's kitchen.

Being an end-of-terrace house, it obviously wasn't very big, but Tazzy had tried to make the most of the space, having had the dining-room and kitchen knocked into one room, a small table at one end at which two people could sit to eat, the rest of the room taken up with the green kitchen cabinets and the Aga she had allowed herself as her only indulgence.

Growing up with her aged aunt in an old, draughty house in Norfolk, Tazzy had come to loathe the idea of ever being cold again. And the Aga burning away all day certainly ensured that the kitchen, at least, was always warm and welcoming.

In fact, the kitten had been curled up fast asleep in her basket beside it when Tazzy and Ross had arrived at the house a few minutes ago.

Tazzy had tried to get Ross to wait outside in the car, still not comfortable with this intrusion into her home, but his request to be allowed to see the kitten made her suggestion seem churlish.

He looked so big in the confines of her kitchen, his head almost brushing the low ceiling, and he had to take great care not to hit the range of copper sauce-pans that hung from a rack from the ceiling.

'She's gorgeous, isn't she?' Ross murmured now

as he squatted down beside her next to the kitten's basket.

Yes, the kitten was certainly a lovely little thing, had actually seemed to recognize Tazzy when she'd come in. At least, she had stretched languorously in her basket and given an almost soundless miaow of greeting!

'Won't you find it a little difficult giving her back?' Ross prompted gruffly.

Tazzy had already thought of that, and knew that she was going to find it incredibly difficult, but if the gold heart-shaped necklace had to go back to its giver—and it did!—then, unfortunately, so did the kitten. She couldn't just pick and choose what gifts she was willing to accept!

'Of course,' she replied. 'But I'm sure you'll agree, travelling as we often do, that it's totally impractical for me to have any sort of pet.'

Ross gave her a considering look. 'Have you always based your decisions on practicality?'

Tazzy felt the warm colour in her cheeks. 'You find something—wrong, in that?' she challenged.

'No, not wrong, exactly.' He shrugged. 'But what about spontaneity?'

What about it? It must be difficult for Ross to understand the lack of it in her own life, being the only child of fairly wealthy parents, and then having been so successful himself as a freelance troubleshooter for any company that needed his assistance with their software—and plenty of them did. But the most recent spontaneity for Tazzy had been whether or not to buy a new winter coat this year or make do with the old one; she had finally decided to make do with the old one!

'Forget I asked.' Ross apologized, seeming to have read at least some of her thoughts. 'That was insensitive of me. It is a pity you can't keep the kitten, though.'

Yes, it was, especially as the kitten had now climbed out of its basket and was padding Tazzy's ankles with velvet paws in an effort to persuade her into picking it up.

Tazzy bent down and scooped the furry bundle into her arms, nuzzling into its fur as it began to purr softly, knowing as she did so that she had already lost her heart to it. Probably because she sensed that the kitten was as much in need of love as she was...

She blinked as sudden tears blurred her vision. This was silly; what on earth was she crying about?

'Don't make any hasty decision about it, hmm?' Ross encouraged as he moved to stand beside her, the kitten's neck arched in ecstasy as he moved a caressing finger against her fur.

Tazzy's breath once again felt constricted—and she knew it had everything to do with Ross's close proximity. Even if it was only so that he could stroke the kitten!

'No,' she agreed huskily. 'I—er—I think I'll just go upstairs and change, after all, if you don't mind?' She thrust the kitten into his arms, moving away abruptly.

'Go ahead.' Ross sat down in one of the kitchen chairs, the kitten on his knee. 'We'll be fine down here. Won't we, Shadow?' He spoke softly to the kitten as it settled itself more comfortably on his knee.

Tazzy nodded tersely in acknowledgement before hurrying from the room, her breathing returning to normal as she walked slowly up the stairs to her bedroom.

It wasn't only the kitten that was throwing her into confusion—Tazzy knew without a doubt that after to-day she would never be able to walk into her kitchen again without sensing Ross's presence there.

Which was precisely why she had tried to prevent her private life and her business one from ever crossing over each other; it was sweet torture to spend every day with Ross and know how much she loved him, but her home had always been the one place she could go to lick the wounds of unrequited love.

But not anymore...

Deciding what to wear to go out to lunch was a little harder than she had thought it would be. On the one hand she wanted to keep her working relationship with Ross as comfortable as it had always been, but, on the other hand, she was conscious of the fact that this was not a business lunch.

Quite what it was, she had no idea, but, on the positive side of things, at least while she was out of the office there couldn't be any more deliveries from her mystery admirer!

Tazzy finally settled on a black sheath of a dress, teamed with the red jacket from a suit she rarely wore to work, on the basis that it was a little too—too vibrant, to wear to the office, especially with her copper-coloured hair.

She looked smart, but still elegantly businesslike, Tazzy decided after one last glance in the mirror before she hurried back down the stairs to rejoin Ross.

'Very nice,' he complimented as she entered the kitchen. 'Smart, but elegant.'

Tazzy felt an inner glow as his words echoed her own thoughts about her change of clothes. Not that she should read too much meaning into Ross's approval of her appearance, but nevertheless—

'Except for your hair, of course,' he added softly.

She gave him a sharp look before moving to stand in front of the mirror hooked on the end kitchen cupboard; she had tidied her hair while upstairs, could find nothing wrong now with its neatness.

'You never wear it down anymore,' Ross murmured as his reflection came to stand next to hers in the mirror. 'I've never forgotten how it looked that day you came for your interview.'

Tazzy couldn't move, barely breathed, could feel the warmth of his body as he stood directly behind her, aware of him with every fibre of her being.

'Such a beautiful copper colour,' Ross continued gruffly. 'With blonde highlights. And please don't tell me those highlights come from a bottle,' he added ruefully. 'I don't think I could stand the disappointment!'

She swallowed hard, trembling slightly at his closeness. 'They don't,' she assured him huskily, her gaze riveted on his reflection in the mirror beside her own.

'Good,' he murmured with satisfaction, one of his hands moving up to start deftly removing the pins that held her hair in place. 'Don't, Tazzy,' he instructed as she would have put up a hand to stop him.

Her hand dropped back to her side, and she was totally aware now of the touch of his fingers against her nape and down her neck, tiny ripples of pleasure moving down the length of her spine as she continued to watch his reflection.

'Better.' He nodded approvingly as her hair fell

down in rippling waves onto her shoulders, his hands—those hands Tazzy so loved!—threading through the fiery strands to loosen them out even more onto the collar of the red jacket.

The effect was startling even to Tazzy, her hair long and silky, emphasizing the deep green of her eyes, her slightly flushed cheeks giving her a beauty that wasn't always apparent.

'Much better.' Ross admired her reflection, his hands resting caressingly on her shoulders. 'How old are you, Tazzy?'

She was way past the stage today of trying to get him to stick to the rules of formality she was usually so insistent on, knew that she was just wasting her time, anyway; Ross was a man who always did exactly what he wanted.

Although quite what he wanted at the moment Tazzy wasn't sure!

'How old am I?' She repeated his question, frowning slightly.

'Mmm.' He nodded, his reflection smiling at her, his thumbs lightly caressing the silkiness of her throat now.

Was it the fact that they seemed to be talking to each other in a mirror that made their conversation take on an intimate note? Tazzy had no idea; she only knew that after this she was going to have a problem maintaining her own side of their businesslike relationship.

'Twenty-five,' she answered him slowly, wondering what her age had to do with anything; unless he was going to point out that at that age she was well on her way to being an old maid, and should perhaps consider her mystery admirer's attention with a little more seriousness!

'That's what I thought. Then why do you do everything you can in order to make yourself appear older? Like wearing this glorious hair confined,' he continued determinedly as she would have protested. 'Very little make-up. And those nondescript coloured suits teamed with white blouses that you always wear to come to work.' He held her gaze in the mirror, those hands caressing the lobes of her ears now.

For exactly that reason! She was all too aware that Ross was twelve years older than she was, that his taste ran to more mature women, usually aged in their thirties, women who knew exactly where the relationship was going—absolutely nowhere!—and were quite happy with that arrangement.

Not that she wanted Ross to think she was at all like those women in that way, she had just thought that if she were to look a little more mature, more confident, he might one day at least notice she was female!

She deliberately broke their gaze in the mirror, moving away from those caressing hands at the same time. 'I had no idea you so disapproved of my appearance,' she said. 'Maybe if you had said something earlier—'

'I don't disapprove of your appearance, Tazzy.' He sighed deeply as he turned to look at her.

'Really?' she snapped. 'It certainly sounded that way to me!'

'If it did, then I apologize,' he told her quietly, his gaze searching.

'I just wondered as to the reason for—for— Well,

for looking so prim and proper.' He grimaced. 'When you can actually look like this.'

'Like this' meaning slightly tousled, her cheeks naturally flushed from the touch of his hands against her sensitized skin, her eyes glittering emerald-green, the dress and jacket giving her a look of slim sophistication!

She gave him a scathing glance, more hurt by his criticism than she would ever let him see. 'I'm your assistant, Ross,' she bit out tartly. 'An efficient one, I hope?'

'Efficiency could be your middle name.' He nodded ruefully. 'By the way, what is—?'.

'Never mind what my middle name is, Ross,' She cut him off, having no intention of ever revealing to him that her middle name had been chosen in deference to her mother's aunt Mabel, the maiden aunt who had brought Tazzy up after her parents were killed in a car crash. Anastasia Mabel Darling; what had her parents been thinking of? 'The point is that I'm your assistant, and as such I dress the part.'

'Yes, but if you just— Never mind.' He obviously thought better of what he had been going to say as he saw the deepening gleam in her eyes. 'I fed Shadow while you were upstairs, by the way.' He indicated the plate of food and saucer of milk. 'So if you're ready, I think we should be on our way to the restaurant?'

'I'm ready,' Tazzy answered him stiffly before picking up her handbag, still smarting from those comments he had made concerning her usual— drab?—appearance.

Surely he didn't want her to look like some over-made-up underdressed vamp when people came to his office, or they went away on business together? If he did, he would have to continue to live with that particular disappointment!

'See you later, Shadow,' Ross murmured as they went out the door.

Tazzy wondered exactly when 'later' he thought he was going to see the kitten again. This was the first time Ross had ever been to her home, and, after his recent comments, she thought it would probably be his last!

CHAPTER FIVE

PIERRE'S was exactly what it sounded like—a very exclusive French restaurant in the most fashionable part of the city. And the proprietor greeted Ross as if he were an old family friend.

As, indeed, it turned out he was!

'Your parents are both well?' Pierre beamed down at Ross once he had personally seen them seated at a table near the window that overlooked the river.

'Very well,' Ross confirmed warmly. 'They're away on a Caribbean cruise at the moment,' he added enviously. 'Can I introduce you to my friend Anastasia?' he continued, at the same time giving her a reassuring smile. 'Anastasia, Pierre.'

To Tazzy's embarrassment she found her hand being taken in the dashing Pierre's before he raised it to brush his lips lightly against her skin.

'*Enchanté, mademoiselle,*' he murmured admiringly.

Tazzy resisted the temptation to pull her hand sharply away as the handsome Frenchman continued to hold it in his grasp long after etiquette dictated he should have released it. Instead she settled for looking around the busy restaurant. 'You're very busy today.' She smiled.

'But of course.' Pierre finally released her hand as he straightened. 'It is the day for love, is it not?' he added huskily, dark brows raised suggestively over sleepy come-to-bed blue eyes.

Tazzy shifted uncomfortably, feeling slightly flustered by such open flirtation. Really! She wondered how this man ever found the time to run a restaurant at all when he possessed such a lethal brand of Gallic charm.

'Not for you it isn't, Pierre.' Ross laughed. 'Get back to your kitchen and give me some space to charm my own girl!'

The Frenchman gave a throaty chuckle of enjoyment. 'As long as you do that, my friend.' He nodded. 'Ozerwise...'

'"Ozerwise," nothing!' Ross continued to smile. 'First things first—could you bring us a bottle of your very best pink champagne?'

Tazzy's eyes widened at the request; she had never drunk champagne in her life, let alone the very best!

'This young lady, she is worth the very best, no?' Pierre said approvingly.

'Yes.' Ross nodded, shooting Tazzy a mischievous grin.

He was enjoying himself! She had found the last five minutes embarrassing, to say the least, the request for champagne completely surprising her, and Ross was enjoying himself!

'You needn't have bothered with a good champagne on my account,' she told him awkwardly once they were alone, the flamboyant Pierre having gone off in search of his very best champagne. 'I wouldn't know the best from the mediocre!' she admitted ruefully.

'Then it's time you did,' Ross told her.

'But—'

'Tazzy, you've had a very unsettling morning, the least I can do is buy you a decent lunch,' Ross cut in firmly.

In truth, she had briefly completely forgotten the events of that morning; being out to lunch with Ross, the owner of the restaurant having obviously assumed she was his lady-love, was much more unsettling than anything else that had happened to her already today!

'Very well,' she conceded. 'But, really, any old champagne will do,' she added quickly, having taken a glance at the menu by now, nearly falling off her chair as she saw the prices quoted next to the champagnes.

Ross began to chuckle, shaking his head as Tazzy looked at him reproachfully. 'Pierre doesn't stock "any old champagne,"' he teased.

'Oh.' She grimaced, once again turning her attention to the menu.

Obviously it was primarily written in French, with English translations underneath—translations that didn't make much more sense to Tazzy than the original! What on earth was—?

'I can recommend the onion soup and the Steak Diane,' Ross told her softly.

Tazzy glanced up at him beneath lowered lashes; had it been so obvious how nonplussed she was by the menu?

Ross grinned at her, his eyes dancing with amusement. 'If it makes you feel any better, his name is really Peter Garstang.'

'Sorry?' She frowned her puzzlement.

Ross leant slightly across the table, lowering his voice even more. 'Pierre,' he enlightened her. 'His name is actually Peter Garstang, and he was born in the east end of London.'

Tazzy turned to look at the owner of the restaurant as he continued to move effortlessly around the room, charming the patrons as he went, that roguish look in his eyes every time he spoke to the women seated at the tables.

She turned back to Ross. 'He isn't French?'

'Not in the least.' He smiled. 'He and I were at school together, that's how I know of his real origins. But what the hell, if it's good for business?'

Indeed. Except… 'That's rather deceitful, though, isn't it?' she said slowly.

Ross gave her a considering look. 'You're very hot on appropriate behaviour, aren't you, Tazzy?'

Was he criticizing her, or complimenting her? She couldn't tell. 'My aunt was,' she answered quietly.

'That will be the aunt that brought you up?' Ross nodded to the wine waiter as he arrived with the champagne.

'Mmm,' Tazzy replied distractedly, her attention on the wine waiter as he deftly dealt with the removal of the cork from the champagne bottle without spilling a drop, pouring a small amount into Ross's glass before standing back.

Ross sipped the pink bubbly wine before signalling his approval, the waiter then filling Tazzy's glass before topping up the first one and then moving discreetly away.

The whole process had only taken a minute or so, and yet Tazzy found herself enchanted by the whole ritual. It certainly beat the carafe of house red that she and Anne usually ordered!

'Aren't you going to try it?' Ross tempted when

the two of them had given their order for food, and
Tazzy still hadn't attempted to drink any of the spar-
kling wine.

She picked up the fluted glass, tipping it up so that
she could drink some of the light pink wine, instantly
starting to sneeze as something tickled her nose.

'Sorry—I think it was the bubbles!' She gasped,
her eyes watering slightly.

Ross smiled affectionately. 'Try again,' he encouraged indulgently.

She did—finding the champagne delicious: light
and bubbly, with a wonderful flavour. 'Mmm,' she
told Ross appreciatively. 'Why pink champagne,
though?'

He eyed her teasingly. 'I could say it was out of
deference to the day!'

'You could,' Tazzy agreed dryly—after the morning she had just had she was well aware of what day
it was!

'But that wouldn't be the real reason?' He gave an
acknowledging inclination of his head at her astuteness. 'Tazzy, I may work with machines all day, but
I do have some romance in my soul, you know,' he
rebuked gently.

Her cheeks felt warm, whether from what seemed
to be his light flirtation, or the effects of the champagne, she wasn't sure. And at this moment, in these
exclusive surroundings, with the attentive but unob-
trusive service, seated opposite Ross at the dining table, bathed in the glow of his undistracted attention,
she didn't particularly care!

'I'm sure you do,' she said warmly.

'The pink champagnes tend to be a little sweeter
than the white, too,' he explained. 'I thought if you

hadn't tried it before you might prefer that to the drier white champagnes.'

But she hadn't told him she had never drunk champagne before until after he had ordered the pink!

Not that it would be too difficult for him to guess that she hadn't; after all, she made no secret of the fact that her social life usually consisted of a trip to the cinema or a meal in a bistro...

'It's lovely,' she assured him.

'Good.' He nodded. 'You were telling me about the aunt who brought you up...?' he prompted softly.

'I was?' She frowned across at him, her brow clearing as she remembered their previous conversation. 'So I was.'

'Don't get me wrong, she was a lovely lady, and I'm very grateful to her for taking me in the way she did—she certainly didn't have to take the responsibility of a five-year-old into her life! But she was already in her fifties when I went to live with her, with rather set ideas about acceptable behaviour. I suppose—well, I suppose some of those ideas were passed on to me,' she accepted heavily.

'Hey, I wasn't criticizing you or your aunt.' Ross reached across the table to rest his hand briefly on hers. 'I find your—code of behaviour, I suppose you would call it...' he smiled '...well, I find it very refreshing.'

'How can such an old-fashioned viewpoint possibly be refreshing?' Tazzy protested, sure that Ross was just being nice to her.

'Oh, believe me, it can,' he assured her with feeling. 'You—' He broke off as their soup arrived. 'Try it,' he tempted as Tazzy looked down at the cheeseencrusted bowl. 'But take care, it will be very hot, and I wouldn't like you to burn your mouth!'

Tazzy suddenly found herself unable to break her gaze away from Ross as his own gaze rested on the softness of her lips, sure this time that she wasn't mistaken, that Ross was flirting with her.

Because it was Valentine's Day?

Because Pierre/Peter had seemed to expect it?

Or could it possibly be because of the obvious attentions of another man, namely her mystery admirer? If it was, if it had finally prompted Ross into seeing her as a woman rather than just his assistant, then maybe all these strange gifts weren't such a bad thing, after all…

There was absolutely no elegant way, Tazzy quickly discovered, to eat the French onion soup; the cheese seemed to have a mind of its own, the onions behaving likewise, and while she was busy trying to tackle the two of them all the liquid ran off her spoon! If it weren't for the fact that the combination of the three was absolutely delicious, she would have given up even trying to eat it after the first few mouthfuls.

'Good fun, isn't it?' Ross chuckled sympathetically as she twirled the melted cheese around her spoon, obviously having the same problem, but completely unconcerned by it.

It was fun, she acknowledged privately. In fact, today was the most fun she had ever had in her life. Made more so, she knew, because she was spending it exclusively with Ross.

'Are your parents enjoying their cruise?' she asked interestedly.

'As I haven't heard a word from either of them since they left ten days ago, I have no idea,' he said.

'But as this month's cruise is by way of being a second honeymoon—to celebrate their fortieth wedding anniversary—perhaps that's understandable. After all, I wasn't even around for their first honeymoon! They were very disappointed you didn't make it to their party, by the way,' he added softly.

The Valentines had celebrated their wedding anniversary two weeks ago by throwing a large party, inviting all their family and friends. And Tazzy.

She had been very touched by her inclusion in their guest list, but at the same time, there had been no way she'd been going to attend. She worked for their son, as a paid employee, and therefore did not belong in their social circle of family and friends. The only person she would really have known, apart from the Valentines themselves, had been Ross, and she certainly couldn't expect him to dance attendance on her when there would be so many other people present that he knew. Or, even worse than that, Ross might have taken his own partner and she would have been forced to watch them together all evening...

She drew in a deep breath. 'It was very kind of them both to invite me—'

'But?' Ross prompted.

She shook her head, not quite able to meet his gaze. 'I did write and tell them that I wouldn't be able to attend because I was busy that evening,' she evaded, knowing that doing her weekly wash, before drying and ironing it, wasn't really a viable excuse.

'Pity.' He shrugged. 'My mother seems convinced it was just an excuse, that the real reason you didn't come was because I'm unkind to you.'

'What?' Tazzy was shocked that Sylvia should ever think such a thing. Especially if the other woman could see just how 'unkind' Ross was being to her right now!

'You don't think I'm unkind to you?' Ross queried huskily.

'Of course not.' She frowned at the very thought.

He raised an eyebrow. 'My mother says I treat you like part of the furniture.'

'But that's ridiculous.' Tazzy gasped her consternation.

'I thought so too—until I sat and thought about what she had said.' Ross spoke consideringly. 'You run my business life so efficiently, Tazzy, that I often forget how disorganized things were before you came to work with me eighteen months ago.' He shook his head. 'Given time, I can fix any problem a computer or its software chooses to throw at me, but my records were in such a mess I often didn't know where I was supposed to go in order to fix the problem. That certainly doesn't happen anymore, now that you put everything on disk and back it up with hard copy.'

'I should hope not.' Tazzy sounded scandalized at the thought.

He looked amused at her indignation. 'My home life wasn't much better,' he admitted with a grimace. 'In fact, I very often had trouble finding a pair of shoes to go out in that matched!'

Ah. Now that was something different...

Tazzy had been absolutely horrified by Ross's complete disorganization when she'd first gone to work for him, but had determinedly concentrated on putting his office in order rather than interfering into his equally chaotic home life. After all, it wasn't in her job description to interfere in the way he ran his personal life.

But the day Ross had been unable to find a pair of socks that had been clean enough for him to go away in had been the day she'd known all that had had to change; it simply didn't give the right impression, computer whiz or not, for Ross to go away on business looking as if he had taken his clothes out of the laundry bag—before they had been washed!

Her first suggestion had been that he get himself a live-in cook/housekeeper; at least then his laundry would be dealt with, and he would be fed on a regular basis—something else he didn't bother with if he was busy.

Unfortunately, when it had finally come to the day of interviewing the three women who had applied for the job, Ross had been called away to deal with a problem that had needed his urgent attention, leaving Tazzy to see the three women instead. Or…perhaps not so unfortunately.

The first woman had been a widow of thirty, with two young children she would have wanted to bring with her. The second had been even younger than the first, single, a tall beautiful blonde, who had been basically looking for somewhere to live in London, and hadn't minded doing 'a little light work' to secure that privilege. Thankfully, the third applicant had been Elvira Brown, a widow of sixty, with excellent references from her last post. Tazzy hadn't hesitated in offering the job to the older lady.

The fact that the first two women had both been young and attractive had had nothing to do with her decision, Tazzy had told herself!

'In fact,' Ross continued, 'Dad seems to be of the opinion that I have all the comforts of a married man without actually being married.'

'I beg your pardon!' Tazzy almost choked on her mouthful of champagne.

Ross looked a little bewildered for several seconds, and then his brow cleared, a grin spreading across his face. 'Anastasia Darling!' he reproved teasingly. 'I'm sure my father didn't mean it in that way at all!'

The warm colour in her cheeks seemed to have become a permanent fixture—although that didn't stop her blushing all over again. Well, in her defence, it had certainly sounded that way to her!

'Sorry,' she finally managed gruffly.

'No need. Perhaps I could have put that all a little more—delicately,' he conceded. 'Dad was really having a go at me because I haven't provided the two of them with any grandchildren that he can "bounce on his knee," was the way he put it, I believe. He seemed to be of the opinion that by the time I get round to it his knees will be too arthritic to support him, let alone any grandchildren!'

Considering that any grandchildren of Sylvia and Nigel Valentine would have to be provided by Ross, their only child, Tazzy found she wasn't too eager for the event herself. If—when, Ross married, she was very much afraid she would no longer be able to work for him; she just couldn't bear to see him with another woman day after day…

'I—' She broke off as a mobile phone began to ring, quickly turning to search through her bag in case it was hers, very doubtful that the charming Pierre/ Peter would welcome this noisy interruption to the calm of his elegant restaurant.

'I think that's me,' Ross said as he took his phone out of his jacket pocket, the ringing immediately becoming louder before he hastily pressed the button to take the call. 'Yes, it is. Yes. Just hold on a minute, will you?' he instructed the caller abruptly, putting his hand over the mouthpiece to speak to Tazzy. 'I'll just go over there and take this call.' He nodded in the direction of a little alcove near the rest rooms. 'I won't be a minute,' he promised as he stood up and moved quickly away.

As far as Tazzy was concerned, he could take his time; she was still recovering from the comment he had just made about him supposedly having all the comforts of a married man. Not all the comforts— there was certainly one 'comfort' of a married man that was missing from their particular relationship!

She was sure that Nigel Valentine had just been teasing his son; his next comment about grandchildren certainly seemed to imply that he had been.

'Why haven't you?' Ross's voice rose agitatedly as he spoke to his caller. 'But you said— He is? Yes. No, I won't be able to do that. Yes, I appreciate that it isn't your fault, but—' He sighed his impatience. 'Okay. Thanks.' He ended the call. 'For nothing!' he muttered as he rejoined Tazzy.

She looked across at him enquiringly. 'Trouble?'

'You could say that,' he said, his expression having taken on a slightly hunted look.

'Anything I should know about?' she pressed; after all, if it was to do with work—

'Definitely not,' Ross stated, sitting back slightly to allow the waiter to remove their used soup bowls, waiting until they were alone again before speaking. 'Tazzy, I—' He broke off, frowning at something over her shoulder.

Tazzy turned to see what Ross was looking at, her eyes widening as she saw a tall, dark-haired man approaching their table in what looked like a very determined way, the man looking extremely handsome in a black dinner suit and snowy white shirt.

He came to a halt next to their table. 'Anastasia Darling?' He smiled down at her warmly, totally ignoring Ross.

Tazzy stared back at the man, feeling very much like a rabbit must do caught in the headlights of an oncoming car—because she had a feeling, a terrible sinking feeling in the pit of her stomach, that something was about to happen that she had no more control over than the poor rabbit did!

Was this him? Was this the man who had been sending her Valentine gifts all morning?

There was no doubting that he was good-looking; probably aged in his late twenties, dark-haired and blue-eyed, athletically fit in the fitted dinner suit.

But the only problem was, Tazzy just knew that she had never set eyes on him before!

CHAPTER SIX

'YOU are Miss Anastasia Darling?' The man looked slightly uncertain now, leading Tazzy to the conclusion that he didn't know her, either. Which meant he couldn't be her mystery admirer. But if not, who was he? And what did he want with her?

'Yes,' she confirmed warily.

'Oh, good.' The man grinned, reaching into the breast pocket of his jacket to pull out a rolled-up piece of paper tied with a red ribbon.

And suddenly Tazzy knew exactly who—what—he was! 'Oh, please, not a kissogram!' She groaned disbelievingly; she had thought she would be safe from her mystery admirer by going out of the office to lunch with Ross at a restaurant—she had obviously thought wrong!

'Certainly not,' the young man said with a smile. 'I am under strict instruction not to kiss you,' he assured her regretfully. 'I am, however, going to serenade you with a love-o-gram.' He untied the piece of red ribbon and unrolled the piece of parchment.

Serenade her—? Before Tazzy could even begin to guess what he had meant by that remark the man had launched into song!

'I love you, Anastasia, with hair of fire and gold, and lips so warm and tender—'

Tazzy couldn't bear it anymore; she buried her face

in her arms as they rested on the tabletop, her shoulders moving emotionally.

The man carried on singing. 'Your legs are long and fine, your waist so curved and shapely, your breasts are so div—'

'Stop right there! Enough!' Ross interrupted loudly, effectively silencing the other man.

Tazzy still didn't look up. She couldn't. And as the other diners in the restaurant began to applaud she knew that for the moment she didn't want to, either!

'More than enough,' Ross stated firmly. 'Thank you,' he added belatedly. 'Now kindly go away,' he ordered.

The applause increased for a few seconds, leading Tazzy to assume that the 'love-o-gram,' having delivered his message, was taking Ross's advice and departing the restaurant.

'Tazzy?' Ross prompted gently. 'Tazzy, are you okay? What a damned stupid thing—' He broke off as Tazzy at last raised her head, frowning as he saw the expression on her face. 'Are you—laughing?' he said disbelievingly, the two of them once more alone at the table.

Of course she was laughing, so much so that the tears were running down her cheeks!

It might be the effects of the unaccustomed champagne, or the craziness of the day, but that—that love-o-gram had to be the funniest thing she had ever heard in her life.

Ross looked astounded. 'But I thought—I thought you were crying.'

'What on earth for?' She still chuckled, taking a tissue from her bag to mop up the tears of laughter. 'Didn't you think it was funny?' She began to laugh again as she thought of the complete absurdity of what had just happened.

'Not that funny, no,' Ross muttered as she couldn't seem to stop the laughter.

'Oh, Ross!' She grinned as she shook her head, once again mopping up the tears. 'It was hilarious! The words were so—so ham, as to render them far-cical!'

He still scowled. 'I'm sorry.' He shook his head. 'I just can't see anything funny about it.'

Obviously he couldn't, leading Tazzy to the con-clusion that she had better stop laughing too. Perhaps it was the champagne, after all. Whatever the reason, it had certainly changed her mind as to the signifi-cance of her mystery admirer; any man that could come up with the words to a song like the one she had just heard couldn't possibly be taken seriously.

'Sorry.' She bit her bottom lip to stop herself smil-ing, aware that her response to the love-o-gram was just increasing Ross's disapproval. 'Still feel sympa-thetic to the man's feelings?' she teased lightly.

He sat forward. 'I—'

'Well, zat was certainly different.' Pierre/Peter chuckled as he came over to their table. 'I was not aware that you were a poet, my friend.' He slapped Ross playfully on the back.

That was the reason Ross was so annoyed, Tazzy realized with a wince; he was frightened the other diners would think he, as her dining companion, had also composed that awful song to her! Why hadn't that occurred to her earlier?

'Oh, it wasn't Ross,' she hastened to correct the other man—and save Ross's blushes!

'It wasn't?' The other man was so startled by this

disclosure that for a moment he forgot his assumed accent. 'I mean, you allow ozer men to seduce your woman?' He frowned at Ross.

A Ross who was obviously squirming with embarrassment!

'But I'm not,' Tazzy said quickly. 'I'm not Ross's woman,' she enlarged as the restaurateur raised dark brows. 'I'm his Personal Assistant,' she explained—and instantly wished she hadn't as the speculation in Pierre/Peter's eyes increased.

Ross gave a low groan. 'Stop while you're not ahead, Tazzy,' he advised. 'As for you, Pierre—go away, will you?' he told his friend irritably.

Pierre/Peter grinned unabashedly as he bent down to speak softly in his old schoolfriend's ear. 'Just one more word of advice, old boy; I don't have a licence for live music, so next time could you—? Okay, okay.' He straightened, holding up his hands defensively, his eyes dancing with merriment at the outraged look on Ross's face.

'It wasn't you,' he drawled. 'But it certainly livened the place up for a few minutes; no doubt the other diners will be talking about it for weeks!' he added wickedly before moving on to the next table.

Tazzy shot Ross a rueful look, wincing as she saw the stony expression on his face. It really hadn't occurred to her until the last few minutes that anyone would assume he had sent her that love-o-gram. No wonder he was so annoyed!

She leant across the table, lightly touching his hand with her own to attract his attention. 'Don't worry about it, Ross,' she soothed. 'We don't actually know any of these people—apart from Pierre, of course,' she said wryly, pretty sure the other man wouldn't forget the incident in a hurry. Or let Ross forget it either, if she had read the other man correctly! 'I know you didn't write that song,' she added consolingly.

Ross focused on her with slightly dazed brown eyes. 'That was, without a doubt, the most awful thing I've ever heard in my life!' he declared disgustedly.

Tazzy straightened, bristling slightly. 'It wasn't that bad! Obviously someone went to considerable trouble—' She broke off, frowning. 'How on earth did he know I would be here…?'

Ross blinked, the same thought obviously occurring to him for the first time too.

'Oh,' Tazzy gasped, biting her lip uncomfortably. 'I told Mrs Brown where we were having lunch,' she explained guiltily at Ross's questioning look.

At least, she thought it was a questioning look; it was difficult to tell when Ross still seemed slightly dazed by the event of the love-o-gram!

Which wasn't so surprising. It really had been the most extraordinary thing she had ever witnessed in her own life, let alone in Ross's. No doubt he was wishing he hadn't invited her out to lunch in the first place!

'That would explain it.' Ross nodded curtly.

Tazzy gave him a considering look. He really did look shaken by what had just happened, more so than she was, actually. 'Would you like to leave, Ross?' she asked. 'I realize this has been—embarrassing, for you.' She grimaced. 'I really don't mind, if you would like to go instead of finishing our meal.'

He straightened, smiling as he obviously made a concerted effort to shake off the events of the last few minutes. 'Don't be silly, Tazzy. We haven't even had our main course yet. Watching Pierre prepare our Steak Diane is an experience not to be missed!' he assured her even as the other man arrived beside their table to do just that.

Ross's prediction proved correct as Tazzy watched in fascination as the other man cooked the ingredients for their meal right there beside their table. Not only did it look wonderful when Pierre placed their laden plates in front of them with a flourish a few minutes later, but it smelt delicious too.

'He may not be French,' Tazzy leant forward to murmur to Ross, 'but he certainly knows how to cook!'

Ross nodded, his good humour seeming to have been restored during the last few minutes. 'Oh, he's the genuine thing when it comes to cooking,' he assured her. 'He trained under a cordon bleu chef in Paris.'

'It shows.' Tazzy nodded before enjoying her first mouth-watering taste of the tender steak. 'Mmm,' she breathed, closing her eyes briefly in ecstasy. 'This is gorgeous!'

Ross watched her indulgently. 'You know, Tazzy, your complete enjoyment of everything is— Well, you're very nice to be around. That didn't come over too well, did it?' He frowned self-derisively.

She laughed softly, shaking her head. 'Don't worry about it. I think I've had more than enough gushing compliments for one day!'

'But— Never mind,' he muttered, turning his attention to his own meal.

Tazzy looked at him beneath lowered lashes. There was definitely something different about Ross today—and she didn't just mean his embarrassment of earlier. Maybe the Valentine gifts, the obvious attentions of another man, really had made him see her as a woman at last; if they had, then even her own embarrassment at the love-o-gram was worth it!

'Is everything all right for you both?' Pierre appeared beside their table once again.

'Wonderful!' Tazzy looked up to glow warmly at him.

Pierre looked at her with admiration. 'Your Personal Assistant, I believe you said…' he murmured to Ross without even looking at him.

'I didn't say at all,' Ross denied. 'Tazzy did.'

'Tazzy…?' Pierre repeated huskily, blue eyes frankly appraising as he continued to look at her. 'How unusual.'

'She's an unusual woman,' Ross bit out curtly. 'Now for the third time today, Peter, will you go away?' he snapped.

His friend turned to give him an amused glance. 'My, my, you are rattled today, aren't you?' he teased softly.

'I'm not in the least rattled,' Ross rasped, glaring up at the other man. 'I'm just asking you to remove your charming presence somewhere else—preferably Outer Mongolia!'

His friend laughed before turning his attention back to Tazzy—a Tazzy who was more than a little puzzled by the exchange between the two men. If she hadn't known better, she would have said Ross was jealous of the other man's marked attention towards her. Which was ridiculous.

For one thing it was obvious that Pierre was charming to all his female customers. For another, for Ross to feel jealous of his friend would imply that he was interested in her himself. And she knew that certainly wasn't true. If his reaction to her mystery admirer was anything to go by, he just didn't want some other man coming along and stealing his Personal Assistant from under his nose!

'It appears that Ross wishes to be selfish and keep you to himself,' Pierre murmured as he lifted her hand to his lips once again. 'I bow to the adage that the customer knows best,' he added with a mischievous twinkle in his laughing blue eyes. 'Might I suggest that the next time we meet it is without the presence of my jealous friend?' he added, giving a mocking bow in Ross's direction before once again taking his leave.

It might all be part of the charming patter that Pierre/Peter indulged in with all his female customers, but even if it was he was certainly doing Tazzy's morale a lot of good. Or maybe it was the champagne that was doing that; whatever, she had enjoyed having such a handsome man flirt with her!

Ross didn't agree, she discovered as she turned back to him, finding herself the focus of his dark scowl.

'What?' She frowned her puzzlement at his behaviour.

'The man's nothing but an accomplished charmer!' he growled.

Very firmly bringing Tazzy back down to earth! 'You're right, he is very accomplished,' she snapped, the colour back in her cheeks.

'But, then, some people might benefit from learning a little charm themselves!' She glared across at him.

Ross frowned. 'Meaning me?'

She shrugged. 'I didn't say that.'

His mouth twisted scathingly. 'You didn't need to! You surely aren't taking any of that rubbish seriously?'

'Of course I'm not taking it seriously!' she returned impatiently. 'Honestly, Ross, what do you take me for?' Her eyes glittered angrily at his obvious criticism; he surely wasn't implying that she had actually *encouraged* Pierre?

If Ross were seriously looking for someone to blame for the other man's flirtatious behaviour, then he should look no further than himself; Pierre was simply responding to what he believed was his friend's display of possession. Which might not be strictly accurate, but Ross was certainly displaying something!

He gave a deep sigh, shaking his head in self-disgust. 'I'm sorry if you think I'm coming on a little heavy, I just—well, I wouldn't want you to take Pierre too seriously, that's all,' he finished lamely.

'I don't think I'm the one that's doing that,' she returned stiffly, his apology, quickly followed by what seemed like yet another insult to her intelligence, doing little to mollify her ruffled feelings.

Ross grimaced. 'Probably not. Let's just forget about it, shall we?'

Tazzy looked at him wordlessly for several long seconds, and then she gave a slow nod of her head. 'Fine,' she said, turning her attention back to her half-eaten meal.

But she was very aware as she struggled to regain some of her previous enjoyment of the food—and failed!—that something had subtly changed between Ross and herself during this lunch-time, that there was a strain between them that hadn't previously been there.

It was a strain she had always feared might happen if they should ever step over that line between employer/employee—and having lunch together in this way was certainly stepping over that line.

She should never have agreed to come out to lunch with him, should never have accepted his invitation. Except…Ross hadn't really made it an invitation, more something that he'd considered was a good idea, and that she'd been expected to go along with.

Well, it certainly hadn't been a good idea—and she didn't know where that left the two of them now!

CHAPTER SEVEN

THEIR departure from the restaurant half an hour later certainly wasn't made any easier by Pierre's parting comment. 'Remember what I said about the live music licence, Ross!' Or the fact that he deftly pulled a single red rose from the vase on the reception desk and handed it to Tazzy as she preceded Ross out the door.

'For goodness' sake, don't take it all so seriously, Ross,' Tazzy finally sighed impatiently. The two of them had driven the two miles back to the house in complete silence, Ross scowling darkly at her side as he parked the car in the driveway.

He turned to give her a rueful glance. 'Lunch didn't turn out quite the way I expected it to.'

She shrugged, inwardly wondering exactly how he had expected it to turn out... 'So let's move on, hmm?'

He gave an appreciative chuckle. 'As easily as that?'

She gave another shrug. 'What's the point of dwelling on something you obviously didn't enjoy?'

'I wasn't the one who was supposed to enjoy it,' Ross protested. 'I wanted to take you out for a Valentine lunch. The love-o-gram, or whatever the man called it—' he grimaced disgustedly '—was a bit of a shock, let's say. And I had forgotten what an affected pain in the butt Peter can be!'

'Don't be mean!' She laughed.

He glanced disparagingly at the red rose she still held in her hand.

'Another one to add to your collection.'

Tazzy looked down at the single red rose, newly in bud, its deep red colour symbolic of the day. She had never received one red rose in her life before today, let alone dozens of them.

'You have this one.' She held it out to him.

And just as quickly wished she hadn't! What on earth was she doing? A single red rose, when given to the right person, was just as significant as the dozens of them she had received this morning. More so, in this case!

Ross looked at the red rose she held out to him, and then up into her face.

A face rapidly suffusing with embarrassment. What had possessed her? What was Ross going to think—?

'Thank you.' He reached out to take the rose gently from her grasp before leaning forward and kissing her lightly on the lips.

Tazzy's lips tingled from his touch, her own gaze completely mesmerized by the gold flecks in the brown of his eyes. Had Ross really just kissed her…?

'I think we can do better than that, don't you?' he murmured huskily, bending his head to claim her lips once more, his arms moving about her as he moulded her softness against him.

She had to be dreaming! Ross couldn't really be kissing her!

But he was. And not just kissing her. But touching her too, his hands moving caressingly across her back.

If she had been standing her knees would have buckled. As it was she just melted against him, melted into him, her arms moving up about his neck as her hands became enmeshed in the darkness of his hair, the red rose crushed between them, forgotten.

His mouth moved searchingly against hers, seeking a response—and receiving it as Tazzy's lips parted beneath his to welcome the kiss.

She had dreamed for months of having Ross kiss her like this, of being able to kiss him; she never wanted this moment to end!

Her spine arched as his caressing hand moved lightly over the firmness of her waist and up to her pouting breast, the nipple hardening against the palm of his hand as he cupped her there, Tazzy groaning low in her throat at the sheer pleasure of having Ross make love to her.

Ross deepened the kiss, his tongue seeking, and finding, the warmth of her mouth, and all the time his hand caressed the pertness of her breast.

Tazzy felt as if she were on fire, the heat pulsing through her body until she hungered for something more, something that was as yet elusive, but that Ross's kisses and caresses promised to fulfil.

He felt so good, so hard and muscular as he crushed her against his chest, only the two of them existing at that moment, no one else—

'Hey, guv'nor!' The call was accompanied by a sharp rap on the car window.

The two of them sprang apart as if they had been struck by lightning, Ross giving Tazzy's blazing face a quick look of apology before he turned sharply in the direction of that intrusive voice, opening the car door to get out to talk to the man who stood there.

Giving Tazzy time to gather her scattered wits together!

What on earth had they been doing? What did she think *she* had been doing?

She should never have allowed their kisses to deepen into such passion, should have called a halt after that first brief touch of their lips. Instead of which, she had given in to the sheer need she had to experience Ross's kisses and caresses.

She had never felt so—so awkwardly uncomfortable in her life!

Not only had they been interrupted by a third person, but how could she and Ross possibly expect to carry on working together after what had just happened between them?

She wasn't sure they could...

Tazzy took a deep breath, tidying the tangles from her hair, giving a regretful glance at the crushed rose, before climbing out of her side of the car to look across at the two men as they talked together.

'Sorry about that, love.' It was the same delivery man who had brought her the box of chocolates earlier this morning. 'I have instructions to deliver this—' he held up a Cellophane-wrapped teddy bear '—at four o'clock today.'

Not another one! was Tazzy's first thought. She would like to tell her mystery admirer to take his teddy bear and—

'Thanks.' Ross impatiently took the bear from the other man. 'I trust you won't be delivering anything else here today?' he added icily.

The man eyed him warily. 'Not here, guv, no.'

'Good,' Ross said with obvious satisfaction.

'Er—I was told to give that—' he pointed to the bear in Ross's arms '—to the young lady.'

Ross moved around to Tazzy's side of the car in two strides, thrusting the bear into her arms. 'There,' he told the other man irritably, his expression grim. 'Satisfied?'

'Er—yes. It's only—' The delivery man looked undecided for a moment. 'Never mind.' He shook his head, his smile more of a grimace as he turned away.

'Thanks,' Tazzy called after him lamely as he climbed back into his van.

'You're welcome,' he told her ruefully before hastily slamming the door and driving away.

Leaving Ross and Tazzy—still clutching the Cellophane-wrapped bear against her breasts!—standing on the driveway...

Ross drew in a harsh breath. 'I shall be glad when today is over!' he snarled before striding across the gravel to let himself in by the front door.

Tazzy slowly followed him into the house, totally miserable now, unsure even what to say to Ross. What could she say to him after what had just happened in the car? *It was a mistake. Let's just forget it.* It had been a mistake. But she doubted that either of them would just be able to forget it had ever happened!

Ross was standing in her office when she entered a few seconds later, and it was difficult, with the irritation still evident on his face, to relate him to the man who had just kissed her with such passion.

'Aren't you going to open that?' he growled, nodding in the direction of the bear she still clasped protectively against her.

'I can already see what it is,' she replied, placing the unwrapped bear on her desktop.

A beautiful honey-coloured bear, at least two feet in height, clasping a bright red heart, with the words 'I love you' emblazoned across it in gold letters. There was also a white card attached to the red ribbon that secured the Cellophane at the top of the bear's head, but at the moment Tazzy was loath to read it. For obvious reasons!

Ross eyed the bear frowningly. 'Someone seems intent on wearing down your defences,' he muttered at last.

Couldn't he see? She didn't care about the bear, or the roses, the chocolates, or the necklace—the jury was still out on Shadow! But at the moment all she really cared about was what had happened between the two of them outside in the car.

'Someone who's too cowardly to even identify themselves,' she dismissed without interest.

Ross looked at her, dark brows raised. 'It seems like a deliberate, and sustained, plan of action to me,' he said.

'It seems like a nuisance to me!' she returned heatedly. 'Ross, about what happened just now—'

'What does it say on the card this time?' He moved to turn the white card over. '"With great affection, and much love,"' he read evenly before turning back to look at her. 'You have to give him marks for consistency, surely?' he drawled.

'After the fiasco earlier in the restaurant, I think he wants shooting!' she muttered impatiently.

Ross shrugged, sitting on the side of her desk. 'Like you, I'm starting to see the funny side of that now.' He grinned.

Tazzy's heart seemed to stop beating at the charm of that grin, her breath catching in her throat as she found herself once again mesmerized just looking at him.

Ross shook his head. 'I'm sure that whoever he is he can't have known how ridiculous that supposed declaration of love was going to be!'

It had been ridiculous, she had said as much herself at the time. And yet a part of her now bristled resentfully at Ross's mockery.

Did he find it funny that another man found her attractive, to the point where he believed himself in love with her? Was that the reason he had kissed her himself, to see what all the fuss was about?

One thing she knew for certain: it was perfectly obvious from Ross's behaviour, since they had entered the house, that he was not about to discuss what had happened between the two of them in the car a few short minutes ago. In fact, he had done everything he could to avoid the subject!

She gave a weary sigh, knowing she needed some time to herself to decide what she was going to do about the situation. It didn't matter how much Ross might try to pretend those kisses they had shared had never happened. They had happened, and Tazzy needed time to think. Alone. In peace and quiet.

'Ross, I have a bit of a headache,' she told him with a frown. 'It's probably the champagne,' she attempted to fib—when in reality the relaxing effects of the champagne had worn off the moment Ross had begun to kiss her. 'Would you mind if I went home early?'

'Not at all.' He stood up, his expression one of concern as he looked at her. 'Would you like me to get you something to take for it before you go?'

'No, thanks.' She turned away to pick up her handbag.

'Sure?' Ross probed worriedly. 'It isn't like you to have a headache, Tazzy.'

It wasn't like her to make a complete idiot of herself by so obviously falling into his arms, either—but she seemed to have done that today too!

'It won't last for long,' she assured him hope-fully—in fact, her temples had begun to throb in ear-nest now.

'Lie down in a dark room for half an hour or so,' Ross advised.

She wanted to bury herself completely in a dark room—for the rest of her life! Anything to avoid hav-ing to come into the office in the morning and face Ross as if nothing had happened.

'I'll bring these out to the car for you,' Ross said, beginning to collect up the gifts she had received throughout the day.

Tazzy opened her mouth to tell him to leave them, and then changed her mind. It might have been these gifts that had sparked off this awkwardness she now felt between herself and Ross, but having them sitting here waiting for her when she came back to work tomorrow would not help the situation.

'Thanks. I—I'll work later tomorrow evening to make up for it,' she offered.

'No need,' Ross refused lightly, the chocolates and teddy bear held firmly in his arms. 'What do you want to do about the roses?' He looked pointedly at the huge vaseful of dark red blooms.

Throw them away! Destroy them! Crush them, like the one they had left abandoned in the car!

'Just leave them,' she told him wearily, sure that she must have had worse days than this—she just couldn't think of any for the moment! 'I—I'll see to them tomorrow.'

She just wanted to leave now, to run away and lick her wounds—to build back her defences so that she could face Ross in the morning!

Ross walked out to her car with her, putting her gifts in the boot before walking round to where she already sat in the driver's seat. 'I'll give you a ring later to see how you are,' he suggested, smiling his sympathy at her.

She didn't want his sympathy! She wanted— wanted—

'There's no need,' she assured him dully.

'I'll call anyway,' he insisted, reaching out to gently touch one of her cheeks. 'You are looking a little pale.'

Tazzy flinched away from his touch; she was feeling too vulnerable, her emotions too exposed, to be able to cope with Ross's gentle concern.

'I'll take your advice and lie down,' she bit out abruptly, firmly closing the car door before he could say anything else, not even glancing his way again as she drove away from the house.

She could breathe easier once she was well away from Ross, her head already starting to clear, her thoughts taking on a semblance of order now that she could look back on the situation logically.

A consequence of Valentine's Day, was what she told herself about the kisses she and Ross had shared. They had been surrounded by love tokens and love messages all day, and Pierre/Peter hadn't helped, with his flirtatious behaviour and his constant hints that she was Ross's lady-love.

No, by tomorrow, with the madness of today firmly behind them, everything would look normal again.

Whatever normal was!

CHAPTER EIGHT

TAZZY stared at the man as he stood on her doorstep, sure that she must have fallen asleep as she lay on her bed, and was now caught up in some sort of nightmare.

The delivery man gave a sheepish smile. 'I only said I wasn't delivering anything to you at that particular house anymore today,' he pointed out. 'I didn't say anything about *this* house!' He held out a large flat package to her, a red ribbon tied decoratively about it.

A package Tazzy made no effort to relieve him of. This simply could not be happening! She would wake up in a minute. And when she did maybe she would find that the whole day had been some sort of horrible dream!

'Go on, love, take it,' the delivery man encouraged. 'It's my last delivery of the day. And I have a wife of my own who expects me to take her out tonight and wine and dine her!' he added with a roguish chuckle.

Tazzy blinked in confusion, at the same time coming to the sorrowful conclusion that she was awake after all. 'Who—?' She cleared her throat, moistening her lips before attempting to speak again. 'Who's been sending me these things all day?' she asked hopefully.

He gave her a knowing wink. 'You should know that better than me, love.'

'But I don't.' She shook her head dazedly.

'Give it a little thought, love,' he advised in a brotherly way. 'I'm sure it will come to you.'

And she was equally sure that it wouldn't!

When she'd arrived home a couple of hours ago she had gone over and over in her head all the men she had even come into brief contact with during the last year, finally coming to the conclusion that it certainly wasn't any of them who were showering her with these gifts.

She frowned at the package the delivery man held. 'This definitely is the last thing you're going to deliver to me today?' She wanted confirmation of that, at least, before she took the ribbon-wrapped package from him.

'Definitely the last, love.' He nodded happily. 'But with any luck, the man himself will turn up before the evening is over!'

Her eyes widened. 'Do you think so?' It was a thought that had never even occurred to her.

'I would have thought it was a pretty safe bet.' The man grinned. 'So, if I were you, I would change into my prettiest outfit and just wait and see.' He pointedly eyed the faded denims and baggy green jumper she had changed into when she'd come in from work.

'Right,' she murmured distractedly, taking the package from him.

Oh, she would be waiting for the man, all right, she might even let him explain himself too—before she hit him over the head with the box she now held in her hands!

Whoever he was, he had caused her more than

enough trouble today, to the point where she wasn't even sure her working relationship with Ross—let alone anything else!—was salvageable.

'Thanks,' she added belatedly.

'You're more than welcome,' he told her warmly. 'I hope you have a good evening.'

'You too.' She smiled, returning his cheerful wave a few seconds later as he drove away.

Well, it wasn't his fault, for goodness' sake, he was just the middleman!

Tazzy slowly closed the door before carrying the package through to the kitchen, placing it on top of the table. 'What do you think, Shadow?' She looked down at the kitten as it rubbed against her denim-clad legs. 'Shall I open it first, or just hit him with it if he does dare to turn up on my doorstep? Hmm—' she nodded '—that's what I think too.' She didn't hesitate anymore but began to untie the red ribbon, standing back with a gasp seconds later as the contents of the box were revealed to her.

Unbelievable!

Unacceptable!

Beautiful…!

Tazzy had lifted the lid of the box to find pink tissue paper, had carefully folded back the tissue paper, to reveal the most beautiful white silk and lace nightgown she had ever seen in her life!

How dared he? had come her immediate thought. Quickly followed by a totally feminine response to something so beautiful: a need to just touch the gown!

She reached into the box now with shaking hands, lifting up the white silk to let it fall down in all its glory.

It really was the most beautiful thing Tazzy had

ever seen, let alone touched, the straps and cups made of pure white lace, the knee-length gown shaped in white silk.

A white card had fallen from between its delicate folds, and Tazzy gently replaced the frothy silk in the box before bending to pick it up. 'Eight o'clock this evening?' the card read.

Tazzy glanced at the silk nightgown, and then back at the card, a deep frown furrowing her brow. If he meant what she thought he meant—!

Who did this man think he was? More to the point, what did he think *she* was? If the implication of the silk gown, and its accompanying message, was anything to go by—!

'Right,' she snapped, folding the tissue firmly back over the nightgown before slamming the lid back on the box. 'Eight o'clock, is it?' she muttered angrily. 'We'll see about that!'

Her headache was certainly forgotten as she sat down at the kitchen table to wait for her so-called mystery admirer, but her head was buzzing with indignation as she constantly glanced at the array of presents she had placed on the table before her: the box of chocolates, the beautiful gold-heart necklace, the still-Cellophane-wrapped teddy bear, the box containing the silk and lace nightgown. And of course there had been the dozens of red roses and that dreadful love-o-gram.

Tazzy's frown deepened as something—she wasn't quite sure what—kept niggling away at the edge of her brain, something that had been said to her today that for some reason she knew was significant. But what was it? And who had said it?

No matter how hard she tried—and she tried very

hard!—she just couldn't bring the memory back into focus. Which wasn't surprising, after the day she had just had!

But it was important. She was sure that it was. Was sure that—

Her head went up sharply as the front doorbell rang, a quick glance at her wrist-watch showing her it was still only seven forty-five. He was early! Whoever *he* was.

No doubt his eagerness had something to do with the silk nightgown!

She could see someone standing on the other side of her frosted-glass front door now, someone tall, dressed in dark clothing, but other than that his form was indistinguishable.

Tazzy moved quietly down the hallway, ducking into her sitting-room—almost like a fugitive in her own home, for goodness' sake! But she intended trying to get a look at the man from behind the drawn curtains in her sitting-room before she actually confronted him on the doorstep—knowing who he was would be of some help!

She drew back with a gasp as she saw it was Ross standing there.

He hadn't telephoned earlier to see how she was, as he had said he would; instead he seemed to have come over personally to make sure she was okay, and, from the dinner suit and snowy white shirt he was wearing, he was going out himself this evening.

He couldn't have arrived at a worse moment!

With her mystery admirer due to arrive any minute, she would have to get rid of Ross as quickly as possible; after reassuring him all day that there really wasn't a man in her life, all she needed was for him to be here when her secret admirer actually arrived!

'Ross!' she greeted him brightly as she opened the door. 'How kind of you to call in this way. As you can see, I'm feeling much better,' she assured him with a smile, at the same time admiring how handsome he looked in his black evening wear—infinitely more distinguished than the young man who had sung her the love-o-gram earlier today!

'As I can see,' he repeated with a perplexed frown.

Tazzy waited for him to say something else—preferably along the lines of 'I'll be on my way, then'—feeling perplexed herself when he didn't.

'You're obviously on your way out somewhere, so don't let me keep you,' she added with casual dismissal, desperately trying not to appear too obvious in her anxious glances past him in anticipation of the other man's arrival.

Ross gave her a quizzical look. 'I'm in no hurry,' he said slowly.

Pity. Or...perhaps not. Perhaps it would be better if Ross was here when this her secret admirer arrived; after all, going on the man's behaviour today, he was slightly deranged, if showering gifts and words of love on a complete stranger was anything to go by!

'Come in and have a coffee, then. Or perhaps you would prefer a glass of white wine?' she offered as he closed the front door behind him before following her down the hallway to the warmth of the kitchen.

'Er—white wine would be fine. Thanks,' he added. 'You certainly seem to have made a full recovery.' He looked across at her, frowning slightly as he sat down at the kitchen table.

'I think it must have been the champagne, after all,'

she dismissed laughingly, opening the bottle of wine to place a poured glass down on the table in front of him before going back for her own. 'A hair of the dog,' she explained ruefully.

More like Dutch courage in order to get through the confrontation that was undoubtedly ahead of her!

She glanced across at Ross, but he seemed rather preoccupied as he stared down into his wineglass. 'Are you going anywhere nice?' she prompted politely, inwardly doing an inventory of the choice of women he could be taking out to dinner this evening. She thoroughly disliked the thought of his spending the evening with any of them!

'I'm not sure yet,' he answered. 'Tazzy—' He broke off abruptly, staring at the array of presents she had placed on the table earlier.

'Impressive, aren't they?' Tazzy nodded in their direction. 'Oh, I forgot, you haven't seen the last one I received.' She moved to pick up the box. 'It is, without doubt, the most insulting thing I have ever been given!' She took the lid off the box.

'Insulting?' Ross repeated with another frown. 'But—'

'There!' Tazzy shook the white nightgown out so that Ross could see it. 'The message with this one read, ''Eight o'clock this evening?'' Can you believe the nerve of the man?' Her eyes sparkled angrily as she dropped the silk and lace back into the box. 'I think he expects me to be wearing that when he arrives!' she added disgustedly.

Ross's eyes widened. 'No—'

'Oh, yes, I think so,' Tazzy continued furiously. 'Needless to say, he's going to be out of luck! How dare he?' She warmed to her subject now, giving vent to the outrage she had been feeling since receiving this last gift. 'He's obviously the sort of man who sends a woman expensive presents but expects something back in return!' She stood up impatiently. 'But he's picked on the wrong woman this time.' Her cheeks were hot with anger. 'And the sooner I tell him that I have absolutely *no* intention—'

'Tazzy, it was me,' Ross cut in softly.

'—of being seduced by expensive presents— *What* did you just say?' She stopped dead, staring down at Ross in disbelief.

He couldn't really have just said—!

Ross drew in a sharp breath, his eyes dark as he looked up at her. 'I said, it was me, Tazzy. I sent the roses and all the other gifts,' he expanded heavily, obviously determined there should be no further confusion.

Tazzy stared at him.

And stared at him.

And stared at him…

CHAPTER NINE

'IT WAS *you?*' Tazzy finally managed to blurt out accusingly, still staring at him disbelievingly.

Ross winced at her obvious incredulity. 'Yes,' he sighed. 'I'm a little early, that's all. So if you're waiting for someone else to arrive at eight o'clock, you're going to be disappointed!' He stood up to move restlessly about the room, his face slightly pale.

Disappointed? *Disappointed!* At this precise moment, disappointment was the least of her emotions!

She was shocked, confused, but most of all hurt. To think that Ross thought so little of her that he had believed she would be seduced by expensive gifts and meaningless words...

'But—but why?' she finally managed to gasp. 'Why would you do such a thing?'

'I— You— Why do you think I did it?' he asked finally.

Tazzy gave a pained wince. 'You don't want to hear what I think!' she assured him forcefully, something else having occurred to her. 'Ross, if this was your idea of a joke, then—'

'It isn't a joke, Tazzy,' he cut in protestingly. 'I—' He swallowed hard, shaking his head. 'I'm sure it's not supposed to be like this!'

Like what? The two of them had worked together for a year and a half now, and, although they had always got on well together, not once during that time had Ross so much as attempted to step over the line of their working relationship. His behaviour today— she still found it hard to believe he was the one who had sent her all those presents and messages!—said he not only wanted to step over it, he actually wanted to obliterate it by making her his mistress, to claim that one 'comfort of a married man' that was so far missing from their relationship!

It certainly made a complete mockery of the love she felt towards him.

'How was it supposed to be, then, Ross?' she asked bitterly. 'Was I supposed to be so overwhelmed by the roses, the chocolates, the teddy bear—? *You* said that earlier today!' The phrase that had been eluding her all evening had suddenly come to her, leaving her more stunned than ever.

Ross had been the one to tease her about the Valentine gift she had received at home this morning. He'd asked her whether the gift had been red roses, a cuddly teddy bear, a box of chocolates, or sexy underwear…!

He had said that because he had known he would be sending her all of those things before the day was over!

As he had delivered the kitten to her doorstep first thing this morning…

'What if Shadow had wandered off this morning before I came out of the house?' She rounded on him furiously, relieved to have something else to vent her anger on; she was still so bitterly hurt that she didn't even want to think about Ross's calculated motivation behind all of this anymore. 'What if he had been run over? What if he—'

'I was parked round the corner the whole time, Tazzy,' Ross assured her wearily. 'I didn't leave until you had taken her safely into the house. It is a her, by the way,' he added ruefully.

He had been there when she'd found the kitten, when she'd looked up and down the street for the person who could have left it, when she'd picked the basket up and carried it into her house...!

She looked at him stonily. 'I want you to leave, Ross.'

'I—'

'Now!' she insisted forcefully, feeling as if her whole world were falling in on top of her. 'And take all your presents with you,' she snapped.

He gave a pained wince at her vehemence. 'Tazzy, if you would just let me explain—'

'But not Shadow. I'm keeping her,' she told him defensively. 'She, at least, is an innocent in all of this.'

'Tazzy, you've misunderstood—'

'I don't think so, Ross,' she said scathingly. 'You certainly aren't the man I thought you were.'

His mouth tightened. 'I'm not the man you think I am now, either,' he grated. 'You're taking all of this the wrong way,' he tried to cajole. 'We've worked together for eighteen months now, and—'

'Not anymore,' she told him coldly, knowing there was no way she could go on working for him under the circumstances. 'I don't know how you came by the impression that I—what signs you could have possibly thought you saw, from me, to encourage today's behaviour—but you were wrong, Ross if you thought any of those *things*—' she made a dismissive gesture towards the presents on the table '—would impress me, would sweep me off my feet to the point where I would listen to any proposal you might care to make!'

He drew in a harsh breath, straightening his shoulders, his expression remote. 'I was—?'

'You most certainly were!' Her eyes flashed angrily.

He swallowed hard. 'In that case, I'm sorry.'

Tears stung her eyes. 'So am I,' she said gruffly. 'I—I really think you had better go now, Ross.' And give her the privacy to let her heart break into a thousand pieces, as it longed to do.

'Yes,' he accepted distantly. 'I— Keep the gifts. Or throw them away. Although I would unwrap the bear before you throw that out,' he added enigmatically before quietly letting himself out by the back door.

Tazzy dropped down heavily into one of the kitchen chairs, feeling totally numb, unable to think, unable to feel, totally lost in the black misery that threatened to engulf her.

And then she reached out an arm and swept all the gifts from the table, crashing them onto the floor, Shadow giving a nervous leap to one side as the chocolates cascaded around her.

'I'm sorry, so sorry,' Tazzy murmured brokenly as she lifted the kitten up into her arms. 'Oh, Shadow,' she groaned before burying her face in the silky fur. 'What am I going to do?' she cried emotionally, the pain she felt inside almost too much for her to bear.

What *was* she going to do? As she had said, she certainly couldn't go on working for Ross, seeing him day after day, knowing that he had thought he could buy her with expensive gifts.

Although even he had looked dismayed by the love-o-gram, she remembered with tearful satisfaction. And no wonder; he surely couldn't have guessed how embarrassing that particular *gift* was going to be!

But the delivery man's enigmatic comment and knowing wink when she had asked for the identity of the giver of the gifts now made perfect sense; he must have known all the time that it was a Ross Valentine, of the same address, who had asked for the deliveries to be made to her. He had probably thought it all extremely romantic!

What could she do? There was no way she could ever pretend today hadn't happened. After this evening's fiasco, she doubted that Ross would want to, either...

What had he thought he was doing? If he had asked her out in the normal fashion, if they had seen each other for a few months out of work, loving him as she did she might have been seduced into a relationship with him. But this—!

She shook her head. Had her love for Ross been so obvious to him? Was that the reason he had thought he could dispense with even the briefest of courtships? It was worse than she had initially thought if that were the case; she had lost her pride as well as Ross and her job.

'But I still have you, don't I?' she told the kitten emotionally as it nestled against her.

A day-to-day reminder of Ross during the long years ahead without him...

The ringing of the telephone woke her early the next morning. Tazzy turned over with a groan to look at the clock on her bedside table, frowning as she saw it was only six-thirty.

No one telephoned at that time of morning unless it was an emergency.

Unless it was Ross, checking to see if she would be going in to work today!

Which she wasn't. How could she, after yesterday?

She had lain awake for hours the previous evening, going over and over each embarrassing event of the day, finally falling into a fitful sleep somewhere between three and four o'clock this morning.

Only to be woken a couple of hours later by this telephone call.

But what if it was Ross? What could they possibly have left to say to each other? More to the point, what could Ross have left to say to her?

She would never know if she didn't answer the telephone call!

'Yes?' She spoke warily into the mouthpiece.

'Oh, you are there, after all,' a female voice answered warmly. 'I thought for a minute— I appreciate it's still early over there, and I obviously can't stay on the telephone for long. I didn't wake you, did I?' Sylvia Valentine added concernedly.

'Not at all,' Tazzy replied cautiously, wondering what on earth Ross's mother was doing ringing her at this time of the morning; as far as she was aware, the other woman was still on a cruise in the Caribbean.

'Good. Only I know that you get up early in order to leave for work on time, and I did so want to be the first to give you our very best wishes,' Sylvia told her excitedly.

Tazzy was sitting up on the side of the bed now,

her head thumping from lack of sleep. Maybe that was also the reason Sylvia's conversation was making no sense…?

'Sorry?' she muttered.

'Nigel and I are so very pleased,' Sylvia continued. 'The two of you are so perfect for each other.'

Tazzy blinked dazedly. 'We are?'

'But of course you are, my dear,' the other woman assured her.

'I knew that from the first moment I saw the two of you together. It's just taken Ross a little longer to see what was always in front of his nose. But I have to say, once he did realize…! Tell me, did Ross get down on one knee?' she prompted with gleeful interest.

Was it possible she was still asleep? Because if she wasn't dreaming, then she really didn't have a clue what Ross's mother was talking about!

'Er—'

'No, that was unfair of me.' Sylvia chuckled softly. 'I'm going to give Ross a ring in a minute, so I'll ask him myself. Is your ring gorgeous? Ross said he had chosen an emerald and diamonds because of your beautiful green eyes.'

Ring? What ring?

'But here I am chattering on, when you must be in a hurry to get to work. And Ross. But I did so want to welcome you into the family, my dear,' Sylvia added sincerely. 'And to assure you that I will be more than willing to help with the wedding arrangements.'

No, Tazzy was still asleep. She had to be.

'If you would like me to, of course,' Sylvia went on quickly. 'Nigel has told me I mustn't interfere, that if you want my help, you'll ask for it,' she confided wryly. 'I'm just so excited about it all.'

Welcome her into the family...? Wedding arrangements...?

Tazzy had missed something, she knew she had. She just wasn't sure what it was!

'I have to go,' Sylvia told her regretfully. 'But we can talk about all of this when we get back in a couple of weeks. We really are so pleased, Tazzy,' she repeated before ringing off.

Leaving Tazzy in a completely numbed state.

That really had to be the strangest conversation she had ever had. Conversation? It had been more like a monologue. A monologue where Sylvia Valentine seemed to be congratulating Tazzy on her engagement to her son Ross!

Someone—and she wasn't sure who—had completely the wrong idea about Ross's behaviour yesterday!

Could it possibly be her who was wrong about him?

But there hadn't been any ring. And Ross certainly hadn't asked her to marry him.

If he had, she wouldn't be feeling so utterly miserable. What—?

She stared at the telephone as it began to ring again. It was too much of a coincidence, too soon after Sylvia's puzzling call, for this second caller to be anyone other than Ross.

Did she want to talk to him?

CHAPTER TEN

SHE most certainly did!

'Tazzy, it's Ross,' he began cautiously once she had grabbed up the receiver. 'I understand my mother has just been on the telephone to you…?'

'Yes,' Tazzy replied just as guardedly.

He gave a heavy sigh. 'I'm really sorry about that. I had no idea— I didn't think— Please disregard anything she said to you that you may have found upsetting.' The grimace could be heard in his voice. 'It didn't even occur to me that she would telephone you like that. But once I had told her how I felt about you she seemed absolutely sure—but never mind that,' he dismissed briskly. 'Don't even think about coming in to work today,' he went on. 'I'm sure you've been bothered by the Valentine family enough for one day.'

'But—'

'I know, Tazzy, your sense of what's right dictates that you should come in to work today,' Ross acknowledged wearily. 'But I really think it's best if you don't.'

She wasn't so sure anymore, felt there were answers she needed to certain questions.

'And don't even think about giving me the ring back—because if you won't wear it then I have no use for it!' he growled before ringing off abruptly.

Two telephone calls. Neither of them making sense. And it wasn't even seven o'clock in the morning yet!

Ross had mentioned a ring too. An emerald and diamond ring? An engagement ring?

There had been a gold heart-shaped necklace in amongst the chocolates, could there possibly have been a ring in one of the other gifts?

Certainly not in with the nightgown, because she had taken that out of the box twice, once to look at it herself, the second time to indignantly show Ross. But if there had been an engagement ring in one of the previous gifts, that snowy white silk nightgown also took on another meaning...

The excitement began to build up inside Tazzy as she hurried down the stairs, the gifts once more on the kitchen table where she had placed them haphazardly after picking them up from the floor the evening before; she hadn't wanted Shadow to eat the chocolates during the night and make herself sick.

The teddy bear!

Ross had advised her not to throw away the teddy bear before opening up the Cellophane and looking inside...

Nestled behind the red heart with the words 'I love you' sewn onto it that the bear held between its paws was a green ring box...

Tazzy's hands shook as she opened up the lid, giving an audible gasp as she stared down at the ring presented in green velvet, a large emerald surrounded by six diamonds...

An engagement ring?

Sylvia Valentine had certainly seemed to think so.

And Ross had implied as much too when he'd spoken to her a short time ago.

But he hadn't asked her to marry him, only to—

No! The ring had been delivered *before* the nightgown, had arrived at four o'clock with the teddy bear, and Ross had arrived at seven forty-five hoping for a positive answer to what was meant to be a romantic marriage proposal. And instead she had thrown him out of the house, assuring him that he had read all the signals wrong if he had thought she would look favourably on any proposal he cared to make to her!

Oh, Ross…

Tazzy looked down once again at the beautiful emerald and diamond ring, tears blurring her vision. Ross might not have proposed yesterday, but he had done everything else he possibly could to show her he loved her: the dozens of red roses, the chocolates and necklace, the love-o-gram, the bear holding this beautiful ring, the white silk nightgown, which she was now sure he had meant as a gift for their wedding night. And all those lovely, lovely messages accompanying the gifts.

Ross loved her!

Not only that, he wanted to marry her!

All she had to do now, she realized, was go to him and tell him there had been a terrible mistake. All! What she really had to do was go to Ross and tell him she had behaved like an idiot, that she had completely misjudged him, and the type of proposal he'd been making.

And hope he would forgive her.

Mrs Brown was busy making scones when Tazzy let herself in by the back door two hours later. 'Mr

Valentine said you wouldn't be in today,' she commented.

'Mr Valentine doesn't know everything,' Tazzy assured the other woman lightly. 'Is he in his office?'

The older woman nodded. 'Been there all night by the looks of him.' She frowned, totally disapproving of the way Ross sometimes became so engrossed in what he was doing that he worked twenty-four hours without a break.

But Tazzy hoped Ross's lack of rest meant he had no more been able to sleep last night than she had.

She had dressed carefully for this meeting, wearing a fitted green dress the same colour as her eyes—eyes the same colour as the emerald ring Ross had bought for her! She had washed her hair, brushing it loosely onto her shoulders in the style Ross had said he liked, applying make-up to hide the shadows under her eyes, blusher to hide the paleness of her cheeks. She only hoped Ross wouldn't throw her out before she had chance to say what she wanted to!

Ross was sitting behind his desk when Tazzy quietly let herself into the room, but he wasn't even pretending to work, his feet up on the desk as he lounged back in his chair, his eyes closed.

But those eyes opened as he sensed her presence in the room, taking his feet off the desk to straighten in his chair, his expression wary as he saw the teddy bear Tazzy carried.

His gaze flickered back to her face. 'I thought I told you I didn't want any of those things back,' he rasped defensively.

Tazzy's heart ached for the lines of weariness beside his eyes and mouth, the slight growth of beard on his face clear indication that he hadn't shaved yet this morning; in fact, he was still wearing the snowy white shirt and black trousers from last night, the dinner jacket draped over the back of his chair.

Tazzy took the green ring box from behind the heart in the bear's paw, holding it out to Ross. 'This is for you,' she told him huskily.

He made no move to take the box from her. 'I don't want it.' He scowled.

He sounded so much like a disgruntled little boy that Tazzy couldn't help giving a rueful smile. 'You haven't seen what it is yet,' she reasoned gently.

His mouth tightened. 'Of course I've seen it—I chose it!'

She shook her head. 'I don't think so.'

Ross's eyes narrowed. 'You think I would let someone else choose what was supposed to be your engagement ring?' he growled.

Her heart gave a leap at these words, her resolve deepening as she placed the box in front of him on the desk. 'I wish you would open it,' she encouraged firmly.

He gave an impatient sigh. 'I told you—' He broke off as he opened the lid to the box, staring down at the ring inside. 'This isn't your ring…' He looked up at her and frowned.

'No,' she acknowledged lovingly. 'It's yours.'

His frown deepened. 'But—'

'I'm wearing mine. See?' She held up her left hand, the ring nestling on her third finger. 'That's your ring.' She nodded towards the open box on his desk. 'From me to you. If you'll wear it,' she added uncertainly.

It had taken her two hours to arrive here after Ross's telephone call, because she'd had to wait for the jewellery shop to open so that she could purchase the ring that now nestled in the box; a wide gold band with their names beautifully engraved on the inside.

She looked at Ross, once again unsure now that she was actually with him. What if she was wrong? What if—?

Ross stood up abruptly, moving quickly round the desk to sweep her into his arms. 'I have no idea what is going on,' he told her ruefully. 'But if that ring means you're asking me to marry you, then the answer is yes!' He groaned before his head lowered, his mouth taking fierce possession of hers before she could gasp a reply.

Did that ring mean she was asking Ross to marry her? She supposed that it did. But what did it matter who did the proposing, as long as Ross continued to kiss her like this?

Which he did, kissing her so passionately that Tazzy's head was spinning wildly when he released her some time later.

'How I love you, Anastasia Mabel Darling!' he murmured emotionally, his forehead resting against hers as he looked down at her with those warm sherry-coloured eyes, his arms possessive about the slenderness of her waist.

'I love you too,' she told him achingly. 'And I'm so sorry I misunderstood what was happening yesterday— You knew all the time that my middle name was Mabel!' She pouted in realization.

He nodded. 'Did I ever tell you that my grandmother, my father's mother, was called Mabel?'

'No.' She laughed softly, so full of love for this man she felt as if she would burst.

'Well, she was. She was also my most favourite

person in the world,' he added huskily. 'Until eighteen months ago, when a certain Anastasia Mabel Darling walked into my life!'

Her eyes widened. 'Eighteen months ago…?'

'Ridiculous, isn't it?' Ross acknowledged self-derisively. 'I think I fell in love with you the first time I saw you. I was just too blind to know it at the time. It took your non-appearance at my parents' anniversary party to show me just how utterly blind I've been all this time.' He shook his head. 'I spent the whole evening moping about as I imagined your ''previous engagement'' was with some other man!'

Tazzy gave him a quizzical look. 'There was no previous engagement and no other man. I just didn't want to spend the whole evening looking at you with some other woman! You see, I've been in love with you for the last eighteen months too,' she admitted shyly.

'Oh, Tazzy!' His arms tightened about her almost painfully as he buried his face in her silken hair. 'The time we've wasted!' He shook his head in self-disgust. 'I would probably have carried on pining away for you if my mother hadn't told me not to be so stupid, that if I loved you I should tell you so and stop wasting time!'

Tazzy felt her previous liking for Sylvia Valentine deepen into a much stronger affection; it wasn't every mother who would encourage her only son in his love for another woman.

'I'm really sorry about her telephone call this morning,' he added. 'Please don't think it was a family conspiracy or anything like that.' He frowned. 'It was just that—before they went away I told my mother—in my infinite wisdom!—that I intended asking you to marry me on Valentine's Day. I don't think it ever occurred to her that you might say no!'

Probably because Sylvia Valentine, with the wisdom of *her* own years, had already been able to see that Tazzy was in love with her son...

'So you decided it was a good idea to bombard me with gifts and love messages on Valentine's Day?' She smiled indulgently.

Ross grimaced. 'I thought I had completely blown it yesterday. What an idiot I was to think you would be impressed with those things!'

'Not an idiot at all.' Tazzy put silencing fingertips against his lips. 'The roses, the chocolates, the necklace...' she touched the delicate gold chain she had fastened about her neck before leaving the house earlier '...even the love-o-gram—'

'That damned love-o-gram,' he groaned. 'I tried to stop it, could see that I had already gone too far with the gold necklace, that you were becoming angry now rather than intrigued, as I had wanted you to be. So I excused myself before we went out so that I could quickly telephone the agency. They said they would try to contact the man and stop him before he reached the restaurant. The phone call in the restaurant was to tell me they hadn't been successful,' he remembered with a wince.

Tazzy chuckled softly. 'Ross, I would have been overjoyed if I had guessed that any of those gifts came from you, even the love-o-gram—'

'I didn't write it, you know,' he put in hastily. 'Merely told them your name and colouring, they said they would do the rest! Hearing that man singing about the beauty of your breasts—! I almost punched him!' he acknowledged grimly. 'As for Peter—!

Despite what I might have said, I had actually booked that table for us two weeks ago. Something Peter was only too aware of.' He scowled slightly at the memory. 'He certainly made me pay for the privilege when he flirted so openly with you!'

He *had* been jealous of the other man. 'There's never been anyone else for me but you,' she assured him as she reached up to kiss him lingeringly on the lips, at the same time revelling in the freedom to do so. 'There never will be,' she added sincerely.

His arms tightened possessively. 'You really mean that, don't you.' It was a statement, not a question. 'That's what I meant yesterday when I said I valued your old-fashioned code of morality,' he told her huskily. 'You seemed to think I was criticizing you in some way, but I wasn't. I want to spend the rest of my life with you, want you with me for the rest of your life, and I know with certainty that if you ever make that sort of commitment to me that it will be for life. I won't settle for anything less!'

'I won't offer you anything less,' Tazzy responded softly.

Ross moved back slightly. 'Tazzy, darling, will you marry me?'

'Oh, yes,' she replied unhesitatingly, her eyes glowing with love as she looked up at him. 'After all,' she added huskily, 'I already have the nightgown for our wedding night!'

'How I love you, Tazzy!' Ross bent to tenderly kiss her lips. 'I love everything about you, your honesty, your loyalty—'

'You make me sound like the family pet,' Tazzy protested laughingly.

'No.' He shook his head firmly. 'Please believe me

when I say I just love being with you. Every moment of every day,' he said gruffly. 'Besides, we already have a pet in Shadow,' he teased. 'It's the family that may need a little working on!'

Her family and Ross's. She could imagine nothing more wonderful.

What a truly miraculous day Valentine's Day was...

FROM BOARDROOM TO BEDROOM

Harlequin Presents® brings you two original stories guaranteed to make your Valentine's Day extra special!

THE BOSS'S MARRIAGE ARRANGEMENT
by *Penny Jordan*

Pretending to be her boss's mistress is one thing—but now everyone in the office thinks Harriet is Matthew Cole's fiancée! Harriet has to keep reminding herself it's all just for convenience, but how far is Matthew prepared to go with the arrangement—marriage?

HIS DARLING VALENTINE
by *Carole Mortimer*

It's Valentine's Day, but Tazzy Darling doesn't care. Until a secret admirer starts bombarding her with gifts! Any woman would be delighted—but not Tazzy. There's only one man she wants to be sending her love tokens, and that's her boss, Ross Valentine. And her secret admirer couldn't possibly be Ross…could it?

The way to a man's heart…is through the bedroom

The world's bestselling romance series.

Seduction and Passion Guaranteed!

They're the men who have everything—except a bride....

Wealth, power, charm—what else could a heart-stoppingly
handsome tycoon need? In the GREEK TYCOONS
miniseries you have already been introduced to some
gorgeous Greek multimillionaires who are in need of wives.

THE GREEK BOSS'S DEMAND
by *Trish Morey*
On sale January 2005, #2444

THE GREEK TYCOON'S
CONVENIENT MISTRESS
by *Lynne Graham*
On sale February 2005, #2445

THE GREEK'S
SEVEN-DAY SEDUCTION
by *Susan Stephens*
On sale March 2005, #2455

**Pick up a Harlequin Presents® novel and you will enter a world
of spine-tingling passion and provocative, tantalizing romance!**

Available wherever Harlequin books are sold.

www.eHarlequin.com   HPTGTY0105

If you enjoyed what you just read,
then we've got an offer you can't resist!

Take 2 bestselling
love stories FREE!

Plus get a FREE surprise gift!

Clip this page and mail it to Harlequin Reader Service®

IN U.S.A.	IN CANADA
3010 Walden Ave.	P.O. Box 609
P.O. Box 1867	Fort Erie, Ontario
Buffalo, N.Y. 14240-1867	L2A 5X3

YES! Please send me 2 free Harlequin Presents® novels and my free surprise gift. After receiving them, if I don't wish to receive anymore, I can return the shipping statement marked cancel. If I don't cancel, I will receive 6 brand-new novels every month, before they're available in stores! In the U.S.A., bill me at the bargain price of $3.80 plus 25¢ shipping & handling per book and applicable sales tax, if any*. In Canada, bill me at the bargain price of $4.47 plus 25¢ shipping & handling per book and applicable taxes**. That's the complete price and a savings of at least 10% off the cover prices—what a great deal! I understand that accepting the 2 free books and gift places me under no obligation ever to buy any books. I can always return a shipment and cancel at any time. Even if I never buy another book from Harlequin, the 2 free books and gift are mine to keep forever.

106 HDN DZ7Y
306 HDN DZ7Z

Name	(PLEASE PRINT)	
Address	Apt.#	
City	State/Prov.	Zip/Postal Code

Not valid to current Harlequin Presents® subscribers.

Want to try two free books from another series?
Call 1-800-873-8635 or visit www.morefreebooks.com.

* Terms and prices subject to change without notice. Sales tax applicable in N.Y.
** Canadian residents will be charged applicable provincial taxes and GST.
 All orders subject to approval. Offer limited to one per household.
 ® are registered trademarks owned and used by the trademark owner and its licensee.

PRES04R   ©2004 Harlequin Enterprises Limited